YOU'VE BEEN AWAY ALL SUMMER

Sheila Hayes

Lodestar Books • *E. P. Dutton* • *New York*

Library of Congress Cataloging in Publication Data

Hayes, Sheila.
  You've been away all summer.

  "Lodestar books."
  Summary: After a summer spent away in Connecticut,
twelve-year-old Fran looks forward to resuming her
usual activities with her best friend Sarah, but Sarah
has a new friend who seems to claim all her time and
attention.
  [1. Friendship—Fiction. 2. New York (N.Y.)—
Fiction] I. Title. II. Title: You have been away
all summer.
PZ7.H314874Yo 1986 [Fic] 85-30756
ISBN 0-525-67182-X

Published in the United States by E. P. Dutton,
a division of NAL Penguin Inc.,
2 Park Avenue, New York, N.Y. 10016

Published simultaneously in Canada by
Fitzhenry & Whiteside Limited, Toronto

Editor: Rosemary Brosnan   Designer: Isabel Warren-Lynch

Printed in the U.S.A.   W   First Edition
10 9 8 7 6 5 4

for Louise, who shared a New York City childhood

1

"Well, Fran, you made it," I said to myself as Mom turned the key in the lock and our apartment door swung open. "You *survived*!"

Okay, so I have a tendency to be dramatic. But so would you if your family had been sliced in two like a bologna sandwich, and you'd been forced to spend the summer in a house where your mother was the cook and where the daughter of the house was world famous as the town snot. I mean, you wouldn't have considered it one long giggle, right?

But here it is, Labor Day weekend, and it turned out just fine. In fact, I may have become quite mature and sophisticated in two months. And Andrea Fairchild (otherwise known as the town snot) is practically a really good friend now. So I think I'm entitled to call myself a survivor. Anyway, I just like the word.

Mom walked ahead of me down the hall, stopping at her favorite room, the first one on the left. She gazed misty-eyed at the familiar scene: the oven, the sink, the Formica countertops. Then she opened the refrigerator and let out a shriek that they must have heard down in Times Square. I thought for a minute that there was a severed head on the shelf, like in a horror movie I saw once. But I should have known better.

"Egads, those people! They looked so nice! How could I have been so naive? How could I have trusted them for a whole summer with my kitchen?" My mother's voice rose steadily as she spoke, and by the time she got to *kitchen,* she was on the verge of hysterics. "Fran, look! There's tofu rotting in my refrigerator!"

I could hear the *thump-thump* of cupboards being opened for inspection as I tiptoed past the kitchen doorway and steeled myself for what "they" had done to my room. But everything was exactly as I had left it at the end of June. It was small (not even half the size of Andrea's) and plain, but it was *me.* I grabbed Herman, the ancient stuffed monkey that sits on my bookshelf, and gave him a hug. Then I heard the front door slam.

"Hey, Ma! When did you guys get in?"

I ran out and hurled myself at my brother. It had only been a month since he and Dad had come up to Connecticut to visit us, but he looked different somehow. Bigger, and older. Almost like Dad.

"Hey, Fran, how ya doin'?"

"Great. Where's Dad? When did you get back?"

"Last night. Dad had to go up to school to get things organized." He looked over at Mom. "Boy, is he excited about getting back to work."

Mom smiled. "I know. He was always ready to get back in the classroom in September, but this year is really special."

"Which reminds me," Steve said, pivoting slowly, like one of those musclemen in the bodybuilding contests, "how do you like the tan? This is a genuine Long Island beach club tan. Do I look gorgeous, or do I look gorgeous?"

"You look gorgeous," Mom agreed.

"Eh," I said.

"Hey, do you know what those creeps did to my room?"

"No, I don't." Mom dried her hands on a towel, shut off the water that was running in the sink, and started down the hall. "I never got past the kitchen," she said. She reached Steve's room and stood in the doorway. "I don't see anything wrong." Then she sniffed loudly.

"See?" Steve said. He was getting a tremor in his voice just like Mom had when she saw the tofu.

I nudged past them and went into the room. "I don't see anything."

"It's not something you see, jerk," he said. "It's something you *smell.*"

"Oh." I smelled. Then I smelled again. "It smells like . . . baby poop."

"Brilliant," Steve said disgustedly.

"Oh, dear," Mom said, putting her arm around Steve's shoulder. I noticed how much higher his shoulder was than it used to be. "Oh, dear," she said again.

Then she glanced at me, and we both burst out laughing at the same time.

"I was afraid they were going to put their baby in *my* room!" I said.

3

"I guess you have to expect this when you sublet an apartment. Actually, all it needs is a little Lysol," Mom said, and at that thought, her mood seemed to brighten. Rotten tofu in the refrigerator, baby poop in Steve's room. These were problems we could handle. The Davies family was together again.

I lugged my suitcases into my room and dumped the contents of both onto the bed.

School was going to start in two days. There was so much to do: I had to unpack; I had to decide what I was going to wear the first day; I had to do some laundry; I had to get school supplies. . . . I had to call Sarah!

I ran to the phone in my parents' room and dialed her number. Busy. I went back to my room and tried to make some sense out of the mountain of tangled clothes on my bed. I hoped Sarah hadn't gotten her school supplies yet. We always go together. Always. But I'd never been away for a whole summer before. Usually, I'd just go up to Merriweather in Connecticut for a week or two to visit Aunt Jessie and Uncle Phil and my cousin Brenda. But this year was different.

Sarah McAuliffe and I have been best friends since the day we were seated next to each other in Mrs. Willerman's first-grade classroom. It was the first time I had really noticed Sarah. She lives two doors down from me, on West Eighty-third Street near Riverside Drive, but up until then, in nursery school and kindergarten, we traveled in different crowds. Anyway,

Sarah has beautiful red hair, and that day she had it pulled up in a bun and tied with a blue velvet ribbon. I remember thinking she looked like a princess. I told her so, and she said she thought my dress was beautiful. It had a puppy embroidered on the skirt, and the puppy had floppy ears and a bell around its neck. I loved that dress, and I loved her loving it, and after that it was a mutual admiration society. Not that we don't have our fights—but most of the time, it's been McAuliffe and Davies against the rest of the world. That's why I'm really ashamed of the way I acted before I left in June.

When my dad lost his teaching job last February, we knew it was only temporary. But even so, there was no money, and when the summer started, Dad took a job out at a beach club on Long Island. Steve went with him and worked as a locker boy. And Mom got the job cooking for the Fairchilds up in Merriweather. I had heard all about Andrea Fairchild's reputation from my cousin. I wonder if I'll ever be able to tell Andrea the part about her being the town snot. Maybe I will, and maybe we'll laugh about it.

But first I had to talk to Sarah. I told her I was spending the whole summer with Brenda. I deliberately lied to her.

I dialed her number again, and this time the familiar voice answered.

"Sarah? It's me. I'm back!"

"Fran! When did you get home?"

"We got into Grand Central about ten, but the traffic coming uptown was wild."

"Gee, I'm glad you're home! How ya been? How was the summer at your cousin's?"

I hesitated a moment. "Fine," I said. "How was your summer? Anything exciting happen around here?"

"Oh, yeah. A rock group moved next door. It's not too quiet, but it's fun."

"Really . . . you're kidding."

"Yep, I'm kidding. Can't fool you!"

"How's Benjamin?" I asked.

"Oh, wait till you see him, Fran. He's a monster. He's the biggest three-year-old in New York City. And he's fresh. He told my mother to shut up the other day."

"Benjamin? I can't picture that! He was so cute the last time I saw him."

"Yeah, but you've been away for the whole summer."

I felt a little dip in my stomach when she said that. It was almost like an accusation.

"Have you gotten any new school clothes?"

"We went shopping the other day, and I got new jeans and a shirt. And I got some neat shoes. But that's all. It's still so hot when we go back, I can't con my mother into a back-to-school wardrobe like I used to."

"I know what you mean. You should see my room, Sarah. I have practically every piece of clothing I own piled on my bed. I'll never finish sorting it out. Did you get your school supplies yet?"

"Yeah. I went yesterday with Marcie. But I'll go with you if you want."

I hoped my voice didn't show my disappointment. A tradition shattered.

"Okay. Can we go this afternoon?"

"Sure."

"Good. Who's Marcie?"

"Oh my gosh, I didn't tell you! Of course you couldn't know about Marcie, you've been away all summer." I didn't say anything, and she went on. "Her name's Marcie Metcalfe, and she's a new girl in my building. The Koniskeys moved. Remember, the old people who lived on the ground floor? They had a little pug dog? Well, anyway, she moved into their apartment, and she'll be going to school with us. She's in seventh grade, too."

"Is she nice?"

"She's great. I'll introduce you. So what time do you want to go get your stuff?"

"Well, I've gotta shovel these clothes around somehow. How about if I come down in about an hour?"

"Super. In front of my house?"

"Right."

"Sure you remember where it is?"

"Come on, Sarah, I haven't been gone *that* long!"

"Only kidding! By the way, how's old Brenda?"

"Oh, she's fine."

"How'd you two get along? Didn't you used to fight a lot?"

"That was when we were little. We got along fine," I said. "Anyway, I'll tell you all about it when I see you."

"Okay. See ya later."

I hung up and went back to my laundry. It was hard to keep my mind on sorting clothes when I was so anxious to see Sarah again, but I had to make it look like I was organized or Mom wouldn't let me out of the house. All the way home, she kept saying how much there would be to do when we got back. I decided to make two piles, clean and dirty, with anything I'd outgrown landing on the floor for Goodwill.

The blue plaid blouse landed on the floor; so did the red T-shirt from Jungle World. Suddenly I was being awfully generous. But everything *was* getting too small for me. I wondered if Sarah had grown much.

Green shorts clean, white shorts dirty, striped shirt clean, blue jeans dirty. Sarah *will* understand why I lied. . . . Sarah *won't* understand why I lied. . . .

Sarah was waiting for me when I got to her stoop. She always gets places ahead of me.

"Hi!" I said, noticing how tall and thin and freckly she was. I wondered if she'd notice my tan. Kids in the city don't usually get a good tan.

"Hi! Hey, you look great. You've got a tan!"

I beamed. "Thanks," I said, falling in step beside her as we headed over to Broadway. "So fill me in. What's been happening?"

"Nothing much, really. Oh—you were right about Charlie Bidwell."

"Oh gosh, what happened? Did he do something terrible to the kitten you gave him? I told you not to! Poor Samantha. To give one of her babies to that creep. What did he do, try to drown it?"

Sarah had stopped and was looking at me. "I had almost forgotten how hysterical you get about everything. I shouldn't have mentioned it."

"Of course you should have," I said, trying to calm down. "Tell me what happened."

"Nothing. I mean, nothing actually happened. His dad caught him in time."

"But something could have happened," I persisted. "So tell me what could have happened."

Sarah let out a sigh. It had been over two months since I had heard one of Sarah's sighs.

"He was doing 'cat experiments.' He was going to throw Midnight out the window to see if she landed on her feet, like they say a cat always does."

This time I was the one who stopped. "Charlie Bidwell lives on the top floor!"

"I know. But like I say, his dad caught him in time."

"So?"

"His dad made him give Midnight back to us, which didn't exactly thrill my mom. But it has a happy ending. Marcie moved in, and her mom let her take Midnight."

"Oh. So how's Samantha? As pretty as ever?"

"Prettier. I think motherhood agrees with her. Except Benjamin keeps teasing her. He tried to ride her like she's a pony, and cats don't particularly like that. Especially when the cowboy's built like a truck."

As we turned the corner onto Broadway, I said, "Let's get some Tofutti! I haven't had any since I left New York."

"You poor thing, how'd you survive?"

As usual, the shop was crowded, but we edged our way over to the counter.

"Strawberry, please," I said.

"I'll have black walnut," Sarah added, same as always. The familiar order reassured me, somehow, that things were back to normal. Nothing had changed.

I looked around, hoping to see the owner of the shop, but he wasn't in sight. I wanted to meet everybody in the neighborhood that I knew and have them really carry on, maybe even cry and scream a little, when they saw that I was home again.

"So you and old Brenda really hit it off, huh? You *must* have, to spend the whole summer together."

"Well, Sarah, to tell you the truth," I began, but the girl came back with the Tofutti, and conversation stopped as we paid and got our change. As we turned and headed out the door, Sarah glanced at her watch.

"It's almost one thirty," she said.

"So?"

"I can't wait to see Marcie. She had a twelve o'clock appointment to get one of those frizzy perms. Can you believe she'd have the nerve? I wouldn't. I mean, her hair is down to *here,*" and she pointed to her shoulder. "But I bet she'll look sensational."

"How old is she?"

"Same as us. Well, no, actually, she's gonna be thirteen in January, so she's a little bit older. She says coming to a new school and starting a new life and all, she can have a whole new look. I think that's a terrific idea. That's the trouble with not starting a whole new life, you get stale."

"You really think moving into the Koniskeys' apartment constitutes a whole new life?"

"Not just moving into the apartment. Moving from New Jersey, for one thing. She says West Eighty-third Street in Manhattan is a whole different planet from

11

Short Hills, New Jersey. And now her mom is a single parent, so the two of them are 'starting over.' She says that a lot. I think it psyches them up."

"What happened to the rest of her family?"

"Her folks got divorced, and she's the only kid. Her dad's still doing his thing in New Jersey."

"What's his thing?"

"Drilling teeth."

"He's a dentist?"

"Of course he's a dentist, Fran. You ever hear of anybody drilling teeth as a hobby?"

We had reached the stationery store, and the icy blast of air conditioning felt good as we went inside. I was beginning to get annoyed that we were spending so much time discussing the altered life-style of this person that I didn't even know. When we reached the aisle where the notebooks and binders were piled in multicolored towers on the counter, Sarah picked up a binder that had a picture of two cocker spaniel puppies on the front.

"Here's the one I got," she said. "Marcie got the one with the daisies. But there's still lots to choose from."

I picked one that had a picture of waves crashing against a bunch of rocks. Then I bought some loose-leaf paper, two notebooks, and a package of BIC pens. We had to stand in line for fifteen minutes to get to the cash register because there were so many kids in the store, but finally we were outside.

"Hey, see back there?" Sarah said, motioning over her shoulder as we left the store.

"Where?"

"Over there . . . darn, you can't see her now. That was Marcie's mom."

"Oh."

"Wait'll you meet her. She's a character."

I let out a huge sigh, but Sarah didn't get the hint.

"She's an award-winning artist. That's what Marcie calls her. My mother calls her a few other things. When they first moved in, she had just gotten her divorce, and she drove my mom crazy. She was always trying to raise her consciousness. *My* mother, can you believe it?"

"Mrs. Fairchild was like that," I said, interrupting as soon as Sarah had paused for breath.

"Who?"

"Mrs. Fairchild. Andrea's mother. She was divorced, I mean. From Andrea's father. But then she married Mr. Fairchild."

"Wait a minute, back up. Andrea's mother . . . who's Andrea?"

Here goes, I thought. "You remember, I wrote you about her."

"Oh! The rich kid that Brenda knew, the one with the country club and the tennis court, and the carousel horse in her room?"

"That's the one. She turned out to be really nice, Sarah. And . . . and Sarah, I have to tell you something." What was I so nervous about? This was *Sarah.* "Promise you won't be mad." Sarah was staring at me intently. "I didn't really stay with Brenda like I told you. My mom worked for the Fairchilds, so I stayed

13

there. But I saw Brenda almost every day," I lied.

"I don't get it."

"You know what a good cook my mom is?" She nodded. "And how my dad was out of work last spring?" She nodded again. "Well, the Fairchilds' cook was going away for the summer, and my Aunt Jessie told them about Mom, and we went there and stayed all summer. And my dad and Steve worked out on Long Island," I finished lamely.

"So why did you say you were staying at Brenda's? Is that what you thought when you left here? That was the address you gave me."

"I know I did. Brenda gave me your letters. No, I knew we were staying at the Fairchilds'. But, well, I was embarrassed. I mean, Sarah, my mom was going to be somebody's cook. You know what I mean. I really hated it."

Sarah didn't say anything as we crossed the street, and I wondered what she was thinking. Was she mad because I had lied to her, or was it just not that important? I wanted to believe the latter. It was so good to be home, and I didn't want to have a fight with Sarah the first day that I was back. I had told her the truth now, so my conscience was clear. I raised my face to catch the warm sun beaming between the buildings.

"So what was it like?" she asked finally. "Did you really live in a mansion?"

"Sort of. It was a big fancy house, anyway. There were fifteen rooms, five bathrooms, and the kitchen was practically the size of our whole apartment!"

"Your mom must have loved that."

14

"Yeah, she sure did. Oh, I didn't tell you, my mom's going to start a business."

"What kind of business?"

"A catering business. Mrs. Karsell—she's this lady who lives in the city, but she was at one of the Fairchilds' parties—wants my mom to do a party for her. My mother's pretty excited about it."

"Will you mind that?"

"Why should I mind that?"

"I dunno, Fran. You minded when she was a cook for the summer, so she's going to be a cook again, isn't she? I mean, it wouldn't bother me, but—"

"It's not the same thing! This is like a regular *career.* Anyway, Sarah, I was wrong before. I know that now. I did a lot of growing up over the summer," I said, hoping she'd notice the little tremor in my voice.

Sarah gave me a shove that almost knocked me over.

"You're so weird, Fran. You haven't changed a bit!" she said, laughing. I felt better about everything when she laughed.

"Anyway, what I wanted to tell you is that Andrea turned out to be really, *really* nice, and I think she's going to come for a visit. I know you two will like each other."

"When is she coming?"

"I'm not sure. I have to write and make it a formal invitation. Her parents are very strict. They hardly let her go anywhere. And they're away a lot, so she gets lonely."

Sarah was playing "count the cracks" as we walked down the block, and I couldn't tell if she was listening

15

or not. But it felt good to talk about Andrea. Maybe I even missed her a little bit, which was silly because I had just left Merriweather this morning. That last thought seemed incredible. I felt as if Merriweather was another world. We had turned the corner and started down our block when Sarah suddenly let out a war whoop.

"Hey, Metcalfe!" she screamed, and took off at a run toward her apartment building. At Sarah's yell, a girl who had been going up the steps turned and started back down. The two greeted each other by jumping up and down and waving their arms frantically.

I came up to them slowly, studying "Metcalfe" as I did. She looked at least sixteen. She was about my height, but more *you know,* and she had shiny dark hair that just exploded all around her head in a jungle of tiny curls. Big silver globes dangled from her ears.

"You look *great!*" Sarah was saying as I reached them.

"Do you really like it?" the other girl squealed. It was obvious that she was crazy about it, and she wanted Sarah to like it, too.

Sarah turned around when I reached the stoop. "Fran, this is Marcie. Marcie, *this*"—and she made a mock bow—"is the famous Fran Davies!"

I felt myself blush.

"Hi, Fran. Welcome back. I've heard so much about you," she said in a high, nasal voice that sounded strangely familiar.

"Really?" I said, suddenly curious. Maybe I *was*

16

missed. Maybe the neighborhood rang with my name for the past two months.

"Come in and see the stuff I got this morning," she said to Sarah.

"You went shopping again?"

I followed Sarah and Marcie into the building. We walked past the elevator and down the lobby corridor to the first apartment on the right.

"Yeah," Marcie was saying as she let us into the apartment, "but I only got a few things."

I realized who she sounded like—that woman in the television commercial who has the terrible sinus problems.

"You've got more clothes than anybody I know," Sarah said. "Fran, wait'll you see her closets."

"Oh, you haven't seen anything," I said. "Andrea had a whole wall of closets, and everything matched and was so neat it was sickening."

"Well, I won't make you sick, I promise. Sarah and me couldn't be friends unless I was a slob, right?" she said, poking Sarah as she went into her room and brought out some clothes. She began to show us a pair of slacks, a turtleneck sweater, and a belt, but I couldn't concentrate on the clothes because I began to notice the apartment.

We were standing on a bare wooden floor in the entrance to the living room, and everything in the room, I mean *everything,* was brown. The chairs, the lamps, and of course all the tables. There were big ugly stone pots all over the place and what looked like a Navajo Indian blanket hanging over the couch. I strained to see, because the room was dark and Marcie hadn't switched on the light, but it seemed to me there was a pile of rocks over in one corner of the room. I felt as if I were standing in a cave. Midnight darted out from under one of the tables and ran past us. She looked totally out of place in this room. I don't know what would have looked at home. A mountain lion, maybe.

"Those are beautiful," I said, turning my attention to the clothes with exaggerated interest.

"She's gonna look so gorgeous, and we'll be our old frumpy selves, won't we, Fran?"

"Yeah," I said, feeling awkward in this mud-colored apartment, with this girl I didn't know, but who seemed to be such a pal of Sarah's. I glanced at my watch. "Hey, we'd better get going," I said to Sarah. "I told Mom I'd be back in an hour. There's a lot to do with just getting home and everything."

"You stay, McAuliffe," Marcie said. "We can watch TV. My mom won't be home till late."

"Okay," Sarah said, going into the living room and turning on a light. I was right: They *were* rocks.

"I'll talk to you later, Sarah," I said. "Nice meeting you, Marcie," I added, knowing I sounded foolish and formal.

"Yeah, you too, Fran," Marcie said. "See you in school."

By the time I had shut the door, the two of them were settled down in the cave, and I don't think they even heard me go. I left the building, hugging my school supplies tightly to my chest. Marcie Metcalfe had spoiled my triumphant homecoming. Now I couldn't be sure that my best friend had really and truly missed me. There weren't even any neighbors out in the hallway to make a fuss over me when I got back to my building.

But as I reached the second-floor landing, I heard my father's laugh coming from the apartment, and as I threw open the door, he yelled "Pumpkin!" in that funny way he had ever since I was a little kid.

I guess someone had missed me after all.

3

Dear Andrea,

Well, here I am, finally writing you a letter! I really intended to write the first night I got back to New York, but you wouldn't believe how hectic things have been. I had to go buy school supplies, and we had to get food, and of course I had to unpack and do my laundry.

So here it is, three weeks later! How have you been? How is school? Do you like your teachers? My homeroom teacher is Ms. Mertle, who was the one teacher I really didn't want to get. Do you think they know that, somehow? Sarah got Mrs. Douglas, who was my first choice. There's a new girl in Sarah's building named Marcie Metcalfe, and she got Mrs. Douglas, too. Anyway, I think seventh grade is going to be really hard, I don't know what you think. Maybe it's different in Connecticut.

Did you ask your folks yet if you can come for a visit? Ask them if you can come for a weekend in October. Please ask right away and let me know!

I have to go now because I've got tons of homework. Bye for now!

Love from your friend,
Fran

Mom says that I should have learned from my experience with Andrea Fairchild not to judge people before I get to know them. And I agree. But Andrea was different. I already know Marcie Metcalfe well enough to make a judgment.

She's not as pretty as I thought she was at our first meeting, but she is kind of interesting looking. And she still looks a lot older than Sarah and me. Partly it's the clothes she wears. I don't think I've ever seen her in anything I'd be allowed to wear before my eighteenth birthday. Okay, so maybe I'm exaggerating. But I'm not exaggerating *much*. All her clothes are really expensive. I know that because the labels are all on the outside. One day I counted, and she had six labels on her. There was one on her shoes, her jeans, her shirt, her sweater, her bag, and her jacket. Count 'em: That's six labels. When I mentioned it to Sarah and she suggested I might be jealous because Marcie dresses so beautifully, I dropped the subject. Anyway, the only other thing I wanted to comment on is her laugh. She's always laughing this really phony laugh. I think if you came up to her and said, "The nuclear missiles are on their way, and they'll be here in eleven minutes," she'd giggle herself to death before they hit.

Other than that, she's a very nice person.

To tell you the truth, I think the thing that really bugs me about this very nice person is not the way she acts or dresses or laughs, but just the fact that she's there. I mean *she's always there.*

It started the very first day of school. I came down to meet Sarah in front of her building so we could walk

21

to school together, the way we've been walking to school together *forever,* and there she was. I thought maybe Sarah was just being nice, because maybe Marcie wouldn't be able to find the school by herself or something, but it's turned out to be a permanent arrangement. There are other kids in the neighborhood who go to our school that she could walk with, but, no, it's become The Three Musketeers.

That first morning she starts off with, "So tell me, Fran, did you really do all those things McAuliffe's been telling me about?"

"Like what?" I said warily, trying to catch Sarah's eye, which was hard to do, since Marcie was walking between us.

"Like the time you rode your bike right into the tree, and when you got up, you had a branch growing out of your ear!" She poked Sarah with her elbow, and the two of them broke into gales of laughter. "And the time you were imitating that teacher's walk, what was his name . . ."

"Keating," Sarah chimed in.

"Yeah, Mr. Keating's walk all the way down the hall, and he was right in back of you, and you didn't know it!"

Sarah had sure picked my shining moments. Hadn't she told Marcie Metcalfe anything good about me?

"I almost did the same thing, didn't I, McAuliffe?"

"Oh, yeah. Fran, listen to this."

"We were over in the park, and do you know the redheaded poet?"

Do I know the redheaded poet? Do I know . . . I

22

discovered the redheaded poet almost two years ago. He comes out in all kinds of weather and recites his poetry to the birds, the squirrels, anything that'll listen.

"Well, I was imitating him," Marcie rattled on, "you know the way he whispers one line, and then hollers the next? And this policeman was standing there, and I didn't realize he was watching me doing this bit, and he really likes the guy's poetry, and . . . well, you had to be there, right, McAuliffe?"

McAuliffe could barely contain her glee. "It was hysterical. You really should have been there, Fran."

I smiled and nodded my head. "Yeah, I guess I should have." But I was in Merriweather all summer. That thought mellowed me a little. So what if Marcie Metcalfe had some good times with Sarah this summer? That can't compare with all we've been through together. Sarah and I are going to room together in college, and when we get married, we're going to be each other's maid of honor. Maybe Marcie Metcalfe doesn't know that yet. I hope I don't have to be the one to tell her.

When we got to school that first day, I expected Sarah to be a little upset at our being separated, but it didn't seem to bother her one bit.

"See you at lunchtime," she called over her shoulder as the two of them started upstairs to Mrs. Douglas's room.

"Maybe we'll have some other classes together!" I cried.

"Yeah, maybe," she answered, as they rounded the stairwell and disappeared from sight.

When I made my way down to the end of the main hallway to where Ms. Mertle reigned like Attila the Hun, the only two people there ahead of me were Jamie Hunter and Jennie Coggins. Jamie is the cutest boy in our grade, and he knows he's the cutest boy in our grade, so it's a standoff: good looks, lousy personality. But Jennie and I used to be pretty good friends. In fact, in third grade, Jennie and Sarah and I hung around together for a while. Then we weren't in the same class in fourth grade, and we drifted apart. That's what happens when you're not in the same class.

That first day I felt the full impact of my new schedule: Nobody was in social studies with me; Marcie was in my math class (which is terrific since that's my worst subject, so she'll think I'm a real airhead); Jennie was in French; nobody was in English; and finally, Sarah and I were together in science and gym. But Marcie has gym with us, so that doesn't really count.

Fridays are getting to be my favorite day, and not just for the usual reason. Marcie takes singing lessons on Friday, so Sarah and I get to walk home together. Just the two of us, the way it used to be.

"So what do you want for your birthday?" she asked me as we got to her stoop on one of those fabulous Fridays.

"Oh, I don't know," I said. "You don't have to give me anything." We always go through this routine, Sarah and I. It's so phony I don't know whether to laugh or throw up.

"You know I'm going to give you something," she said. "We've exchanged presents every birthday since

24

we were seven, so don't be stupid. Would you like some jewelry?"

"Yeah," I said greedily, the formalities over with. "Maybe one of those green hearts like Annette has."

"Aren't they pretty? She got it in Johnson's. I saw it there. It comes in red, blue, and pearl, too. I think the green one's supposed to be emerald."

I shook my head. "I think it's supposed to be jade. Emerald's bright and shiny."

"How do you know?"

"Andrea's mother had an emerald ring"—I made my fist into the shape of a baseball to show Sarah how big it was—"and she also had jade earrings. So I learned the difference."

"It really impressed you, didn't it?" Sarah said. I couldn't tell if she was annoyed or just curious.

"Not really. Well, maybe a little." It was funny. I had hated going, I had dreaded Sarah's finding out the truth, and now it seemed like an adventure I wanted to share with someone.

"Have you heard from Andrea?" she asked.

"Not yet. I wrote and asked her to come for a weekend in October. I hope she can. I want you to meet her. I know you'll like her."

"I don't know. She sounds awfully la-di-da to me."

"She is not. She's real nice."

"If you say so."

"Did I tell you my mother's business is really getting going? She's running around like crazy, and she's complaining a lot, but I think she's pretty excited about it."

"That's nice. Listen, you want to go shopping tomorrow? You know there's only four days left before your birthday."

"I know," I said, grinning. "I'd love to." We always go shopping for presents together, and then we pretend we're surprised when we open the box. It makes a lot of sense. That way you always like what you get.

"I have a dentist appointment in the morning," Sarah said, "so how about if we go in the afternoon? About one?"

"Great. Call me."

I heard Mom rattling things around in the kitchen as I opened the door. "Hi, I'm home!" I called. No answer. I poked my head in the kitchen doorway. Mom was hustling back and forth from the refrigerator to the stove, holding a piece of paper out in front of her. "Hi, I'm home," I repeated.

"Hi, sweetie," she said absentmindedly. Then she went back to reading the recipe. She looked up at me finally. "Another friend of the Karsells called. A party on the seventeenth. A *big* party on the seventeenth. I'm going crazy."

"That's great. Aren't you excited?" I asked, but Dad came in before she had a chance to answer me.

It used to be, Dad would come home and tell Mom all about his day, and Mom would listen intently and not say very much. It was almost as if she didn't have a day of her own to talk about. Now she starts babbling as soon as he comes in. Today she was telling him about a meeting of some women's group she had gone to (which she had heard about from that gal they met at the Block Association meeting the other night.

26

. . . Didn't he remember? The artist with a loft in the Village? Of course he did!), and *they* had suggested she place an ad in the *Women's News,* and that's what she was going to do!

Then Dad said wasn't she rushing things a bit? What if she got more work than she could handle?

And Mom said fat chance of that happening, but anyway this artist—C.B., Mom called her—said if that happened then Mom could afford to open her own place just like the professionals do.

I got the impression Dad wanted to go sit down and read the paper, but he kept standing in the doorway nodding his head and saying things like "Really?" and "That so?" and "Sounds good."

Mom looked really flushed by the time she was finished. I don't know whether it was from the excitement or from poking her head into the oven every few minutes to check on whatever it was she was cooking.

I tried a few times to interrupt and tell them how I was going shopping with my best friend Sarah McAuliffe tomorrow for my birthday present. But I couldn't get their attention, so I just left them alone and went into my room.

Anyway, sometimes it's more fun to keep good things to yourself for a while.

I had just finished my dinner when the phone rang.

"FRAN!" My brother always brays like a mountain goat when the call is for me, as if we lived in a canyon instead of a six-room apartment. I think he just gets mad that it's not for him. Nobody wants to answer the phone when it's not for him.

"You don't have to *shout,*" I screamed, taking the phone from him and moving it out into the hall. We have two phones; one is in my parents' bedroom, where my dad's always working, and the other's in the kitchen, where my mom's always working. So if I want any privacy at all, I have to move the phone out into the hall. Sometimes my brother hangs around to listen, and then I have to take it into the bathroom. When I'm grown-up and rich, I'm going to have telephone extensions in every room in the house.

I cradled the receiver under my chin while I shut the bedroom door and settled myself on the floor in the hallway. I figured it was Sarah. She always calls on Friday night after dinner.

"Fran? It's me, Andrea. Andrea Fairchild."

"Andrea! How *are* you?"

"Fine. How are you?"

"Oh, *fine*," I said.

There was a pause, and neither of us said anything for a moment. I was so surprised to hear from her. And so glad. Why was it so awkward?

"Did you get my letter?" I said finally, pleased that I had thought of something to say.

"Yes, I did. Thank you so much. I've been meaning to answer you, but I'm a terrible letter writer."

"Well, did you ask your parents if you can come for a visit?"

"I tried to hint about it, Fran, but you know how they are. Richard would have a fit. But that's why I'm calling! I want to ask you—are you busy tomorrow?"

Tomorrow, Saturday. Shopping with Sarah.

"Uh, not really. Why?"

"Well, I know what next Tuesday is, and Richard and Maggie are coming into the city for a meeting tomorrow, and they said I could come in with them and meet you for lunch. My treat, for your birthday."

"Oh, wow! That would be great. But you don't have to treat."

"Don't be dumb. It's for your birthday, of course I have to treat. Where would you like to go? How about the Russian Tea Room?"

"The Russian Tea Room?" I'd heard of it, and I'd even passed it a few times, but I'd never actually been there. The social chasm between Andrea and me opened up once again. But we had crossed it last sum-

29

mer; we could cross it again. "I've never been there,"
I said, "but I've heard it's great."

"My folks eat in the Tea Room all the time because
their office is nearby , but I've only been there twice."

"Can we go by ourselves?"

"Of course we can. Like I told you, my father practically *lives* in the place."

"Well, great!" I said.

"Can you meet me there at twelve?"

"Sure," I said, getting really excited.

"Maybe we'll see some celebrities. Last time I was
there, I sat right next to Elliot Gould, but that was no
big thrill. Remember that funny scene in *Tootsie?*"

"I didn't see it."

"Oh. Well, there was a scene where Dustin Hoff-
man dresses up like a woman—I mean, that's the
whole point of the movie—and he follows his agent
into the Russian Tea Room. Of course, the agent
doesn't know it's him, but then he recognizes him and
he says, 'Oh God, Michael, I *begged* you to get some
therapy!' It's a riot. I mean, he thinks Dustin Hoff-
man's gone bananas because he's dressed like that."

I laughed, but it didn't come out sounding real.

"You had to see the movie," she said with a sigh.
For some reason, *that* sounded really funny to me, and
I started to giggle.

"I'm sorry if I'm talking too much," she said.

"Don't be silly. I'm really looking forward to seeing
you again."

"Have you changed much?"

30

"Yeah," I said. "I look like Christie Brinkley now."

"I don't think I want to see you after all."

"No way! You're not getting out of it!"

"So I'll meet you at twelve out in front. You know where it is, don't you?"

"Sure. Fifty-seventh Street between Sixth and Seventh Avenue. It's right next to Carnegie Hall."

"Right. So, I'll see you tomorrow."

I hung up the phone and sat back on my heels. Lunch at the Russian Tea Room! It sounded so elegant. I jumped up and ran down the hall to tell my mother.

"Mom, that was Andrea Fairchild."

Mom was kneading dough and reading a recipe that was fastened to the cupboard over her head. She turned and gave me a quick smile. "That's nice. How is she?"

"She's fine. And Mom, she wants to take me to lunch tomorrow at the Russian Tea Room, for my birthday!"

"Hey, that'll be fun. What are you going to wear?"

"I never thought of that!"

I spent the next hour putting together what I considered a Russian Tea Room outfit. My denim skirt, button-down shirt, a vest, argyle knee socks, and loafers. I wish I had the green heart already, I thought. Then I remembered Sarah. I'd have to break our date to go shopping. I felt kind of bad about that because we always went birthday shopping together. Maybe we could go earlier.

I called her, and when I explained about Andrea, there was a big, fat silence on the other end of the phone.

"Oh," she finally said.

"I was thinking maybe we could go shopping earlier, in the morning?"

"I have a dentist appointment. Remember, I told you."

"Oh . . . I forgot. How about later on in the afternoon?"

"I don't know. I think I have to baby-sit for Benjamin."

"Oh."

"Well, have a good time with Andrea," she said.

"Thanks. Bye now."

I hung up the phone and sat staring at it. I knew Sarah pretty well, and there was something about the way she said *Andrea* that made it sound like a contagious disease. For a moment, I didn't feel like going to meet Andrea. I wanted to call back and make things right with Sarah. Then I remembered that she had gone and bought school supplies with Marcie Metcalfe. That had always been something we did together, too. She broke *that* tradition. I thought about the Russian Tea Room again. Andrea said celebrities go there for lunch. . . .

I stepped off the bus at the corner of Fifty-seventh Street and Broadway, crossed the street, and walked down to Seventh Avenue. While I waited for the light,

I looked down the block. There it was. First, the plain brown canopy that said CARNEGIE HALL (like it wasn't a very important place at all) and then next door to it, in snazzy red and white, THE RUSSIAN TEA ROOM.

I hurried over to where Andrea was waiting.

She seemed taller than I remembered, and she had that neat-as-a-pin appearance that had so turned me off in the summer. She was wearing an absolutely smashing Ralph Lauren outfit: pink and gray plaid, with everything coordinated, right down to the belt. Right away I had to remind myself how much we had grown to like each other before. And I had to forgive her all over again for being pretty and rich and well-dressed.

"Hi!" she said as she spotted me and came over.

"Hi!"

There was an awkward pause while I tried not to notice that she was holding a little gift in the same hand with her shoulder bag.

"Come on, let's go in," she said, turning and opening the door.

The front of the restaurant was lined with red leather banquettes that Andrea passed as she walked up to a woman at a small desk. She sure seemed to know what she was doing.

"Fairchild reservation," she said crisply.

"Ah yes," the woman said, checking the list in front of her. "Right this way, Miss Fairchild."

We followed her into another room where she led us to a table against the wall.

"And how is your father these days?" the hostess asked pleasantly as Andrea slid into the leather seat against the wall.

"Fine, thank you," she said, smiling.

I couldn't believe how poised Andrea was in situations like this. I trip over my own feet entering the school lunchroom.

The waiter brought us each a menu and left. The menu was huge, and everything was written in Russian. I stared at it a moment and then looked across at Andrea. If she could read Russian, this friendship was going to end right here. But she giggled when she saw the expression on my face.

"The translations are on the back page. See," she said, flipping the menu over. I did the same, and sure enough, there was the menu in English. I began to study the list of dishes.

Andrea took the small, gift-wrapped box and placed it in front of me. "I hope you like it," she said.

"Oh, Andrea, you shouldn't have!"

"Why not?" she asked, staring at me in that direct way of hers. "We're friends, aren't we? And friends give each other presents on their birthdays, don't they?"

I thought fleetingly of Sarah, and I wondered: Could you add a good friend? Or did each new one mean an old one had to be discarded? I'd hate that.

"Thank you so much," I said.

"Go on, open it!"

I tore at the purple ribbon, trying not to damage the

34

little violets that were fastened to the top of the box. When I opened it, all I saw at first was a cloud of lavender tissue paper. I unfolded it carefully, and there it was: a small, painted box, the kind I love to keep on my dresser. I picked it up and examined it carefully. The sides were gold, and the top looked like it was made out of crushed pearls. In the center of the top, there was a painting of a carousel horse.

"Oh, Andrea!" I looked up at her, and the pleased look on her face told me that she knew how much I loved it. "It's gorgeous. But it looks so . . . you know . . ."

"Expensive? It's not really. Richard's company made these to give away with their cosmetics, one of those 'bonuses,' you know? So I can have as many as I want," she said matter-of-factly. "I thought of you when I saw this one, and since you wouldn't let me give you the real carousel horse from my room, I figured this was the next best thing."

"Thanks so much," I said, placing it carefully back in the box. "So how *are* your folks?" I asked.

She raised her eyebrows. "You know—busy, busy. They just got back from Majorca. Doesn't that sound like the most exotic place in the world?"

I nodded. The waiter was at my elbow.

"Would you young ladies like to order now?"

I looked back at the menu in panic. I hadn't even gotten halfway down the page.

Andrea looked up at him. "I'll have the chicken Kiev. Fran? You like chicken, don't you?"

I grunted.

"I think you'd like this. It's boneless chicken stuffed with butter and herbs, and it's fantastic."

"That sounds good," I said, glad to be relieved of having to decide.

"What would you like to drink?" she said. "I'm going to have a Coke."

"I'll have the same."

It reminded me of the story Mom tells about her and her sister, my Aunt Jessie. When they were little and went out to a restaurant, Aunt Jessie always ordered whatever Mom ordered. Right down to the dessert. Mom says it was like an echo.

Andrea was craning her neck to see all around the room.

"Do you see anybody?" I asked.

She nodded. "Yeah. Herman Gluck and his wife."

"Who?"

She stared at me, and we both started to laugh. The people at the next table turned and looked at us. For a fancy restaurant, the tables were squeezed awfully close together. If a movie star came in and sat next to me, I'd practically be in his lap. When the people kept staring at us, that set us off. The more we tried not to laugh, the more we laughed. I tried taking a drink of water, but that was a mistake; I spit some out, and it almost landed on Andrea's plate. We finally calmed down as the waiter arrived with our food, but the laughing had helped. I was really relaxed with Andrea again. What had taken the whole summer to achieve was now accomplished in about an hour. Our relationship was definitely making progress.

"Mmm," I said, with my mouth full of food, "you were right. This is delicious!"

We ate in silence, enjoying the taste of the buttery herbs and chicken. I was wondering if I could get the recipe so my mother could make it at home, when I noticed Andrea's eyes growing wide as she focused on something over my right shoulder. The way we were sitting, she was facing the whole restaurant; I was facing Andrea and the wall.

"What is it?" I asked. She didn't answer, so I repeated, "Who is it?"

"Adrienne. It's Adrienne Richards!" she said, in a stage whisper.

I looked at her blankly. "Who's Adrienne Richards?"

"Sometimes, Fran Davies, I think you have the brain of a hen. Adrienne Richards? 'Live for Tomorrow'?"

"Oh—ADRIENNE RICHARDS!" I hadn't intended to scream, but the excitement of my delayed reaction overwhelmed me. Adrienne Richards was one of the leading characters on "Live for Tomorrow," the number-one soap in America. I peered over my shoulder and finally spotted her against the opposite wall. She was wearing a light blue suit with a white ruffled blouse. Very un-Adrienne. The last time I had watched "Live for Tomorrow," Adrienne was in a jail cell wearing a shapeless gray sack and waiting to hear if she would get a new trial. She had been convicted of murdering Nathan Truffles, the playboy. As I stared across at her, the busboy came and cleared away our plates. Then the waiter appeared.

"Would you care for some dessert?" he asked.

Andrea looked over at me, but I just shook my head. I didn't feel as if I could eat another thing.

"We'd just like the check, please," she said.

Andrea belonged in a place like this, I thought. She's so cool. Regular, but cool. I'm just regular.

Every once in a while, I looked over my shoulder to see what Adrienne Richards was eating. First, she had a glass of white wine, then she had a salad. Then the waiter came and handed Andrea a slip to sign.

"Thank you very much, Miss Fairchild. I hope you've enjoyed your lunch."

"Yes, we did, thank you," Andrea said as we got up to leave. As we passed through the other room, I could see her searching the tables for another celebrity. "Richard and Maggie are picking us up at one thirty, so we're right on time."

"Us?"

"Well, they have to pick me up, and we'll be going up the West Side, so I thought we could drop you off."

"Sure," I said as we waited outside. "I didn't realize they had driven in."

"They used the limousine. Richard hates to drive in the city."

As she spoke, the biggest car I'd ever seen in my whole life drew up to the curb, and Mr. Fairchild stepped out and waved to us. Andrea hurried over, and I followed.

The limousine was drenched in Mrs. Fairchild's perfume. It was called Dragon Scent, and the Fairchilds' company made it. The fragrance brought me right back to Merriweather and the summer and the Fairchild mansion.

"Charles, we want to drop this young lady off. What's the address, Fran?" Mr. Fairchild asked.

I gave it to him, and as the limousine pulled away from the curb, he settled back and turned toward me, saying, "It's quite nice over there now, isn't it? Glad to see the West Side making a comeback." He began to talk then of when he was young and living in the city. "Couldn't live here now, I don't think. Though we're always talking of getting a little pied-à-terre. No, I've gotten used to breathing fresh air!" he said, and he laughed that brittle laugh that I also remembered from the summer. He was wearing a tweed jacket and a shirt opened at the neck with a red and gold paisley scarf tied around his throat. I wondered what kind of a meeting he had that he could go dressed like that. But, of course, when you're the boss, I guess you get to dress any way you want. That's another nice thing about being rich.

As we turned in to Eighty-third Street, I began to search the block for somebody I knew. I really wanted Sarah, or better yet, Marcie Metcalfe, to see me getting out of a limousine.

As if on command, the door to their apartment building opened, and Sarah and Marcie emerged with Benjamin between them. I started to wave as we pulled up to the curb, but it wasn't necessary. They both took a good long look at the limousine and who was inside. Then as Charles got out to come around and open my door, they turned their backs and headed toward the corner.

I thanked Andrea again and waved to the Fairchilds as they pulled away.

It had been such a good day. The lunch was fun, and I loved the present Andrea had given me. Sarah and Marcie's laughter drifted down to me as I stared for a moment at their backs. Why was Sarah being so childish? I had never realized how immature she was. Maybe I just noticed it now because I was becoming more sophisticated. *I* had just had lunch with Adrienne Richards at the Russian Tea Room.

A few scattered leaves from the Drive blew across my path as Mrs. Sadowsky from 4G came out to walk her schnauzer.

"Hello there, Frannie. What have you been up to today?"

She said the same thing every time we met, but today she had hit the bull's-eye. She wasn't as good as Sarah, and not nearly as good as Marcie, but I was desperate.

"Well, Mrs. Sadowsky," I began, "*guess* where I had lunch!"

"Have you written Andrea a thank-you note?" Mom asked, passing me a piece of carrot cake.

"A thank-you note? Mom, that's only for Grandma and Aunt Jessie. I can't write Andrea a thank-you note!"

"And why not? After all, she took you for such an elegant lunch."

"I'm writing her a letter. Is it all right if I just stick the *thank-you* in there somewhere?"

My mother looked at me and shook her head. "I guess so."

"That Andrea Fairchild sounds like a real snob," Steve said.

"She is not! You met her when you came up for a visit, remember? She's real nice!"

"Yeah? Then why'd she take you to a fancy place like the Russian Tea Room? If she was really your friend, and she just wanted to see you, you would have gone to Burger King."

"I don't know, Steve," Mom said, "I think Andrea wanted to make it a special treat for Fran's birthday, just like we took Fran to Dobson's on her birthday.''

"Yeah," I said, "I didn't notice you cringing at the door, saying, 'No, no, I want to go to Burger King.' "

Mom and Dad laughed, and Dad said, "Hoisted by your own petard" to Steve. He always says that when somebody starts an argument about something and ends up losing it.

"Hey, Mom, this tastes funny," Steve said, making a face as he swallowed. "It doesn't taste like it usually does."

"Okay, so I ran a little low on a couple of things and had to improvise. I didn't think you were such a gourmet that you'd notice."

"Wasn't it also—pardon me for mentioning it—*frozen?*" Dad said. My dad doesn't like anything that's been frozen. He was grinning like he was only fooling, but I knew deep down he was serious. I hate it when my folks do that: Make a joke about something *in front of the children,* but you know they really mean it.

"Hey, you two, you're lucky you got a home-baked dessert. I'm a working woman now. Pretty soon it's going to be Sara Lee for all of you."

"Is your business really that good?" I asked.

My mom nodded. "It's really beginning to take off. Maybe I *shouldn't* have run that ad!" she said, giving Dad a funny look, as if this were a little joke between them.

"I told you this might happen. You've only got a small kitchen, you know. You'll get in over your head, Margaret."

"Then I'll have to expand, like C.B. said. Look for space to rent outside."

Dad shook his head and put on what Mom calls his wise-old-owl expression. He usually uses it when he's explaining some homework to Steve or me. "Honey, you're going much too fast."

Suddenly, Mom didn't look so chirpy. "What do you mean?"

"I only mean that I'd hate to see you take on more than you can handle."

Mom stared at Dad for a moment. Then she got up and started to clear the table. I was thinking of having another piece of cake, but I guess it wasn't meant to be.

"It's very clear that *you* don't think I can handle very much," she said to Dad.

"Oh, come on," he said, sounding exasperated.

Mom went into the kitchen and started banging plates around the way she does when she's upset. She never used to get upset very often, but since we've been back and she's been trying to get her business started, she's become a semi-professional plate banger. She also wears her glasses all the time now. She's had them for a couple of years, and she used to wear them only once in a while, when she was reading very small print. But lately she's always working over a list, or reading a recipe, or making notes, and wearing her glasses.

Mom stuck her head back into the dinette and said, "You know, C.B. warned me something like this

43

might happen, but I laughed at her. I laughed at her!"
she repeated.

I went in to help. "I'll do the dishes," I said. "Why
don't you go and sit down?" And make up with Dad,
I wanted to say. But she didn't answer. She was running the water in the sink, and she pretended she
didn't hear me.

I can't stand tension. When I grow up, I'm going to
have tension headaches, I know I am. Right now, it just
makes me nauseous. Not nauseous enough to stop
eating, but nauseous. I started putting things away in
the refrigerator, being careful not to use too much
aluminum foil. I didn't want to do anything to set Mom
off again.

Finally I said, "I think it would be terrific if you
rented some space and really got a business going."

My mother finished washing a pot, then turned the
water off and dried her hands slowly. "Oh, I don't
know. I haven't really thought it through yet. I know
it's probably much too soon, and we don't have the
money, but as C.B. says, 'If you're going to fly, you
have to flap your wings!' She's always saying things
like that. She's so encouraging. *Not like some people I
could mention,*" and she shot my father a look as she
switched off the kitchen light and went down the hall
into their bedroom.

I followed her. "Who's this C.B. you're always talking about?"

"She's a gal like me, starting a career. But her husband was totally unsupportive, so she's divorced
now," Mom said, raising her voice. I guess she wanted

my father to hear her all the way out in the living room. "She's got this tremendous energy and drive. That's what I need. I've been a dull, frumpy housewife too long."

"You're not dull and frumpy!"

"Well, compared to her I am."

"Does she live around here?"

"Right in Sarah's building. I'm sure I told you, Fran. She has a daughter in your class."

"A daughter in my . . . what did you say her name was?"

"Connie Beck."

I breathed a sigh of relief. "I don't know anybody named Beck."

"That's her maiden name. She uses it professionally. She's an award-winning potter."

I jumped off the bed. "Mom, she's from New Jersey, isn't she!"

"Yes, she is. Short Hills."

"Mom, you *can't* be friends with Marcie Metcalfe's mother!"

"That's her daughter's name. Marcie. I couldn't think of it."

"Mom, she's . . . she's a *character.* "

"When did you meet her?"

"I didn't. Sarah told me."

"Well, aren't you two the little gossips. Actually, she's an original, invigorating kind of person, so don't be judgmental. Now, I've got to get back to work or I'll be up all night making pâté for the Henderson thing."

I went into my room and took out my science note-book, but then I went back out to the kitchen. "What'd you say she was? An award-winning what?"

Mom looked at me blankly over her glasses. "An award-winning potter."

"What's that?"

"Oh, you know, Fran. A potter is someone who . . . pots."

"You mean they make things like big, mud-colored stone jars to put around a living room?"

"Yes, I suppose so."

"It figures," I said. Then I went back into my room and tossed the science notebook on the floor.

I took out the box of stationery that Sarah had given me for my birthday. She said they were all out of green hearts when she finally went shopping. I think that's where she was going with Marcie that Saturday. She said she wasn't sure what other color I'd like, so she thought the stationery was a better idea. It's lovely stationery, with little pink flowers all around the border. And now that I've got a friend to write to all the time, I'll really need it. But I was really looking forward to having that green heart.

Dear Andrea,

Here I am writing you a second letter, and you haven't even written me one *yet! But I forgive you because you gave me such a great birthday present, and because I had such fun at the Russian Tea Room. Thank you so much!*

It was very nice seeing your parents again. Your mother looked so beautiful!

So when are you going to come and see my parents again? Please ask your folks if you can come for a visit. My mother would love to see you, and I know we'd have fun. Really **beg!** *Thanks again for the lunch.*

Love,
Fran

P.S. My mom has become a working mother just like yours now, and she's making a lot of new friends. In fact, now she's friends with the mother of my best friend's new friend. It sure is a small world!

I started to add *too small,* but then I erased it.

Sarah hadn't seemed at all surprised that my mother knew Marcie's mother, or that Marcie and her mother had different last names.

"Honestly, Davies. You're so *antique,*" was the way she put it. This was something new with Sarah, calling me by my last name. I didn't like it.

"Well, I don't understand why Marcie's laughing all the time when her whole life's been chopped up like chicken liver."

"Haven't you ever heard about creative divorce? It was probably the best thing for all concerned."

"I dunno. Andrea's folks were divorced, and she missed her father so much. She never gets to see him anymore. He lives in California now, and he's remarried—"

"I know, you told me."

"All I know is, it would make me feel awful. I mean, how would you feel if you and your mom went off and left your father with Benjamin?"

Sarah let out a hoot. "No chance. My dad won't even take Benjamin to the hardware store. He says Benjamin walks too slow."

"All I know is, Marcie Metcalfe must be a very shallow person not to feel bad."

"Jeez, you're so depressing, Davies. You're not happy unless somebody's miserable. So her parents got divorced. Big deal. Half the kids we know have parents who're divorced."

"Not half."

"Almost. David, and Arlene, and Robby."

"And Lauren," I added.

"Yeah, and Tommy Spence, and that kid who used to sit behind you and throw spitballs. What was his name?"

"Jason?"

"Yeah. His dad married somebody who posed for *Playboy*. Did I tell you that?"

"No! Where'd you hear that?"

"Around. Everybody knows it."

"*I* didn't."

"You've been away."

That made the seventh time Sarah had said that to me.

I will never learn to count to ten before I bite into a slice of pizza.

"What's the matter?" Marcie asked, staring at me as tears ran down my cheeks and I took huge gulps from my Coke.

"Burned the roof of my mouth," I gasped.

She nodded imperceptibly, with a little intake of breath that made it very clear that she thought I was a moron. "I don't see why you guys want to spend a gorgeous afternoon in a museum. That is so dumb," she said, rolling her eyes as she took a cool, ladylike bite of her pizza.

Sarah didn't say anything.

"We don't want to, but we have this dumb project for Mr. Vanderet. What can we do?" I said.

"Do it some other time."

"We can't. We're late as it is." I looked over at Sarah, hoping to see her nod in agreement, but she was too busy unraveling a string of mozzarella that was threatening to strangle her. I guess I was the only one secretly pleased that we had to do this project. The way I looked at it, anything we got to do without Marcie tagging along was like a birthday party.

We finished the pizza and spent ten minutes deciding how much to tip. I know you're supposed to tip fifteen percent, but sometimes that's hard to figure.

"Just leave a couple of bucks," Marcie said, running her fingers through her tangled hair. Her silver earrings shook like little Christmas ornaments when she tossed her head.

"That's too much," I said. "Let's see. Seven dollars and fifty-two cents. So seventy-five cents would be ten percent, and a dollar fifty would be twenty percent. Somewhere in between?"

"How about a dollar twenty-five?" Sarah volunteered.

Marcie sighed loudly. *"Finally,"* she said.

We came out of Luigi's into the glare of brilliant autumn sunshine.

"So long," I said to Marcie as we headed for the corner.

"C'mon, let's go sit on the Drive for a little while," she said. "You've got time."

"We can't, Marcie, we told you. This report is due on Monday. Maybe we'll see you later." But as we started to walk away, Marcie fell into step alongside. "You're coming with us?" I asked, not even trying to keep the annoyance out of my voice.

"Might as well. Nothing else to do."

"Great," Sarah said, "the more the merrier."

Funny. I always thought it was two's company.

We made our way over to Central Park West and down to Seventy-ninth Street, where the American Museum of Natural History stands like a fortress overlooking the park. As we climbed the steep steps leading to the entrance, I could hear Marcie mumbling beside me.

We paid the student rate at the admission booth, and I wondered why Marcie was spending money to go in somewhere that she didn't want to be. I guess she just had to be included in everything.

"Where do we want to go?" I asked Sarah, as we passed through the turnstile into the cavernous stone entrance hall.

"Back outside," Marcie said.

Sarah giggled, but I ignored her. "I'll find out," I said.

"Dinosaurs are on the fourth floor," the woman at the information desk told me.

We rode up in the elevator and got off and turned

to the right, stopping at the first doorway to stare up at three dinosaurs stationed on a platform in the center of the room. We went in and looked closer.

"That one looks like Mr. Vanderet," Marcie cracked.

Sarah laughed, but I didn't. Mr. Vanderet was boring, but he didn't look at all like the dinosaur.

"Do you have the project paper?" I asked Sarah. I was determined to ignore Marcie Metcalfe and make her feel like the outsider she really was. Sarah dug the mimeographed sheet out of her bag, and we began to read the information on the plaque at the base of the platform: GREAT DINOSAURS OF THE JURASSIC PERIOD.

"This guy's not the one we want," Sarah said.

"This guy's not the one *anybody* would want," Marcie said. "Even my mom wouldn't go out with him," she said, grimacing.

I glanced over at Sarah, but she was reading the sheet and didn't seem to notice Marcie's remark. Why was I always so sensitive? Maybe Sarah was right. Divorce could be *fun*.

"Let's check down the hall," Sarah said, starting along the marble corridor. We had begun to follow, when Marcie stopped at a wall display of dinosaur bones.

"Look at this," she said. "Gross me out!"

I kept going, anxious to close the distance between Sarah and me. That's what I seemed to be doing all the time now, ever since I got back: trying to close the distance between Sarah and me.

"Here they are!" Sarah shouted as she rounded the corner. The woman selling pamphlets at the end of the corridor gave us a look over her glasses. There were only a few other kids around, so who did she think we were disturbing, the dinosaurs?

There were four more skeletons on display here. I read the plaque under the display, then opened my notebook and began to write:

TRACHODONTS . . . Late Cretaceous Dinosaurs.
The skeletons grouped on the central island in this hall represent dinosaurs that once lived together in western North America. . . . They were among the last of the dinosaurs to live on the earth. . . . The four skeletons in this group belong to three well-known genera of late Cretaceous dinosaurs. . . .

Suddenly a purple sneaker clamped itself over the sign, blocking the words. Marcie was standing on the platform. She had climbed over the railing and had her arm around the dinosaur's neck.

"Marcie, get off there!"

Sarah was doubled over with laughter. "How can you stand to touch that thing!"

"Marcie, get down, you'll get in trouble," I whispered, looking frantically around to see where the guard was.

Marcie laughed and began to step over the wooden railing that protected the display. But at that moment, the guard appeared in the doorway, and all three of us saw him at the same time. Marcie caught her foot on the railing and went sprawling.

While we helped her up, the guard hurried over. He looked furious.

"How dare you climb on a display. You should know better than that!"

"It was an accident," Sarah sputtered, "and she's hurt."

Marcie was hugging her knee, and she looked like she was about to cry.

"Did you hit your knee when you landed?" I asked.

She nodded. Then she stood up and put some weight on her foot. "Nothing better be broken, or I'll sue this place," she said to the guard.

He glared at her.

"Shut up!" I hissed.

"The three of you'd better leave," he said.

"Oh, but I'm not finished," I began.

He smiled a tight little smile. "Oh, yes, you are," he said.

"What a grouch," Sarah said as we headed for the elevator.

"Little creep! Just wanted to flaunt his authority. Made him feel important to throw kids out. My knee hurts!"

I turned and looked at her. "Marcie, why did you climb up on that thing? I mean, that was really dumb!"

"Fran, she was only horsing around. She didn't break anything."

"But we were thrown out! And this project is due on Monday. The whole day's been wasted."

"Now we can go to a movie!"

"No, we can't," I said. "I don't have any more money."

"I have. I'll treat."

"What's playing?" Sarah asked.

"I don't know. Who cares?"

"No thanks," I said, "I'm gonna start home."

"Oh, come on. I didn't get you out of that mausoleum just so we could all go home."

I stared at her. "Did you do that on purpose?"

She grinned and rubbed her knee. "Well, I didn't intend to break a leg."

Sarah gave her a shove. "You're crazy!"

"You guys sure you don't want to catch a movie?" Marcie asked.

"Yeah," Sarah said. "I should get home, too. I told my mom I'd baby-sit if I got back in time."

"I'll baby-sit with you," she said.

"Okay."

"You want to come, too, Davies?" Marcie asked.

I stared straight ahead into the park as we descended the steps. "No, thank you," I said finally. "I have some things to do."

"It's just as well," Sarah said. "My mom doesn't like me to have a crowd over when I'm baby-sitting."

We hardly spoke to each other the rest of the way home. Now I was a crowd.

7

It hadn't been the worst school day I'd ever had. That was still a tie between the day Richie Zarro told everybody he'd seen me sitting on the toilet in kindergarten, and the day in fourth grade that Linda Barnes and her group decided to run two contests—a beauty contest, which, of course, Linda intended to win, and a "plain Jane" contest, which she very sweetly encouraged me to enter because there were going to be *real prizes*. How that girl escaped having a peanut butter and jelly sandwich squeezed up her nose, I'll never know.

To get back to today: First, I got yelled at in chorus because I was talking to Billy Stewart. I laughed like it didn't bother me, but it always bothers me when I get yelled at in front of a large group of people. Next, I got a seventy-eight on my French test. I've really been working on my French, so as they say, it was *très* disappointing. And then, of course, the real clincher: Sarah and Marcie sat giggling together all during assembly. I was supposed to be sitting with them—I mean, the three of us were supposed to be sitting together—but we weren't together at all.

So it was with a heavy heart that I came into the

apartment and threw my books down on the table. And then I saw it. I didn't recognize her handwriting, because I don't think I've ever *seen* her handwriting, but the return address in the upper left-hand corner was clear. I ripped open the envelope.

Dear Fran,

Thank you for your very nice second letter. I guess you think I'm terrible for taking so long to answer, but I was hoping I could write back with some good news. But I'm afraid I can't. It's nothing personal, and I hope you and your parents understand that, but Richard doesn't want me spending time in the city when he or Maggie isn't there with me. I really don't think my mother would mind, but she goes along with everything he says. I'm so sorry.

The winter stretches ahead dark and dreary, and I know it sounds corny, but I miss the summertime when you and your mom were here. Well, maybe lightning will strike, and he'll change his mind!

Thanks for asking, and write again soon.

Your friend,
Andrea

I sat there a minute, holding the letter and staring out the window into the dirty windows of the building across the street. I was so disappointed that if I'd been a little bit younger I swear I would have bawled.

The key clicked in the lock, and I turned as my mother came bouncing in the door. I choose my words carefully; I now have a mother who *bounces.* A bouncy mother in glasses.

"Hi, toots. What's up?"

It's like a bad dream. Sarah calls me Davies, and Mom calls me toots (or sweetie, or hon). Whatever happened to plain old Fran?

"Hi." I followed her into the kitchen and started unloading the groceries to see what good snacks she had brought in. Skim milk, oranges, tofu, watercress, some kind of lettuce, and toilet paper. "Didn't you get any cookies?"

"You eat too many cookies, hon. Anyway, there're some in the cookie jar."

"They're raisin cookies, and they're stale. Why don't you bake some?" I asked.

"Now? Are you kidding? I've got to throw a casserole together for supper, and then work on the Stevensons' party. I have to whip up something really exotic for them. The theme of the party is birds—any ideas?"

"That's easy. Put feathers in everything."

"Ugh! You're a big help."

I sat down on the kitchen stool and nibbled on a stale raisin cookie. Mom must have noticed my face, finally, because she said, "What's the matter?"

"I got a letter from Andrea. She can't come."

She stood still and thought about that for a moment. "That's a shame. But maybe the timing's not right, anyway."

"What d'you mean, the timing's not right?"

"Well, I'm getting so busy, for one thing. And I was looking at your room the other day. After the Fairchilds', it looks pretty scrungy."

"Andrea wouldn't have minded." Suddenly, my

58

mood brightened. "Hey, were you thinking of redecorating my room?"

"Maybe. C.B. has some wonderful ideas. She's made me realize that we shouldn't be living in an environment that's so hostile."

"So *what?*"

"So hostile. To our needs, to our sensibilities. Since C.B. is an artist, she knows a lot more about this sort of thing. She said your room could be stifling to a person your age."

My stomach started to flip-flop. That whole Metcalfe/Beck family was out to get me. "I don't want Marcie's mother to decorate my room," I said.

"Why not? She's really much more creative than I am. And anyway, she wouldn't be decorating. She would just be giving me some guidance. You know I'm no good at that sort of thing. Her apartment is delightful. Have you seen it?"

"Of course I've seen it!" I snapped. "It's weird. It's awful. You wouldn't want an apartment like that, would you?"

"Now, hon, you've got to broaden your tastes. What's wrong with their apartment?"

"Well, first of all, it's mud-colored, and there're stone jars all over the place and big blankets hanging on the walls. It reminds me of a cave."

Mom laughed. "Fran," (Hurrah, my name!) "C.B. is a potter. Naturally, there's an earthen influence to her home."

I stared at my mother. "You cook. You don't decorate with spaghetti and meatballs, do you?"

59

"That's ridiculous."

It was like that science fiction movie, *Invasion of the Body Snatchers,* where aliens take over people's bodies. They look the same, but they don't act the same.

"I don't want Marcie's mother to touch my room," I said.

Mom looked at me for a moment and then tossed the dishcloth she'd been using into the sink and went into her room.

"Fine," was all she said.

When the doorbell buzzed, I went and looked through the peephole.

"It's me, Connie Beck."

I opened the door, and the first thing I noticed was her jet black hair. It hung down almost to her waist. The next thing I noticed was her "shades." In the dark apartment hallway, she was wearing sunglasses.

"Hello there," she said, walking right in without waiting to be invited. "You must be Fran, right? Marcie talks about you all the time."

I had to bite my tongue to keep from blurting out, "What does she say?"

C.B. marched ahead of me down the hallway. She was wearing a long suede skirt, brown boots, and a striped Mexican poncho. She looked just like her apartment, and I knew right away I didn't like her.

Mom met us at the kitchen doorway. "Hi. Want some coffee?"

"God, I need something after the afternoon I've had. You didn't come to the meeting."

"I couldn't. I had too many other things to do."

"You're going to be left out of the decision-making process if you keep that up."

"I don't know how you get any work done with all your politicking!" Mom said, placing two cups of coffee on the dinette table.

"I cannot believe how naive you are, Margaret." She spoke slowly and deliberately, the way a person might speak to a small child. "My work *is* political," she went on, "*your* work is political too. Every time I put my hand to clay, I'm making a statement about the impurity of life; every time you mash a potato, you're making a statement about violence."

She stopped to take a sip of her coffee and blow some cigarette smoke into Mom's face. My mother just sat there like she was in class. She didn't blow the smoke away or cough or anything. I don't remember: In that movie, did the aliens come from New Jersey?

I went into my parents' room and dialed Sarah's number. While I waited for her to answer, I thought about how my mother, who was too busy to bake cookies, wasn't too busy to sit and have smoke blown in her face by Marcie's mom.

"You'll never guess who's here," I began, when she answered.

"Who?"

"Marcie's mother."

"That's nice." I could tell Sarah was thinking "So what?" If I had said *Marcie,* she'd have been annoyed, and maybe even jealous. But she didn't care if my mother was pals with Marcie's mother.

"My mom wants her to help decorate my room because my mom thinks she has terrific taste." There was silence for a moment, and I held my breath.

"Oh, you poor thing!" she said then, and we both burst into giggles. "I hate Marcie's house," she whispered, as if she was afraid Marcie would hear her all the way from her apartment.

"So do I. I told my mom it looks like a cave."

"Exactly. Or a mud hut. Does she really like that stuff? Your place always looks so nice."

"All of a sudden, my mom doesn't think so. She wants to redo my room so it won't stifle me."

Sarah let out a shriek. "Are you kidding me?"

"No! Honest."

"Boy, I'm sure glad my mother isn't friends with Marcie's mom."

"Now I think she's mad because I said I didn't want them to touch my room."

"Good for you. I've always liked your room."

"Thanks. It's not fancy, and in a way, I'd love to do it over. But I'd do it sort of frilly, like Andrea's. Her room was gorgeous. It had a canopied bed and thick green carpeting—"

"And a carousel horse. I know, you told me. You keep talking about that place like it was so great. I thought you didn't like it."

"I don't know," I said. "When I was there, I thought I was miserable. But it hasn't been so hot since I got home." She didn't say anything, and I was afraid she'd realize that I meant the way she'd been acting so friendly with Marcie, so I quickly added, "Anyway,

I got a letter today. Andrea's not even coming. Her folks won't let her."

"That's too bad. I was getting kind of curious to meet her." There was a pause. "So I guess you're stuck with me, after all."

"Sarah?" I said. "Let's not fight anymore, okay?"

"That's fine with me."

"Good. So, I'll see you tomorrow?"

"Right."

"So long, Sarah," I said.

"So long, Davies," she said, and we hung up.

8

In my dream, someone had heaped huge globs of vanilla ice cream all over the city. Everything was covered with it: the cars, the parking meters, the windowsills. It was a neat dream, and I was really enjoying it, when I opened my eyes and saw what looked like huge chunks of white bread streaking past my window. It really *was* snowing.

I looked at my alarm clock as I tumbled out of bed: 8:30.

Mom was in the kitchen drinking coffee.

"Did we get a snow day?" I asked.

"Nope. I just forgot to wake you up this morning."

"Ha, ha, very funny." I went over to the living-room window. Just as in my dream, everything was under a mantle of snow. "Isn't the beginning of November awfully early to have this much white stuff?"

"*I* think so," my mother said. "That's probably why you got a snow day. They weren't ready for it."

"This is terrific. I can get my sled out. Hey, you're home, too!" I said as Dad came down the hall in his pajamas.

"Yes, I am, unfortunately. Morning classes were

canceled, but I'll have to get there this afternoon."

"I wouldn't count on it," Mom said. "The city's pretty much at a standstill."

"Well, I'll walk then. I have to give these notes to Dr. Gerson."

"If it's so bad out, will he be able to get there?" I asked.

"Good point, Fran," Mom said, grinning.

"Dr. Gerson lives one block from the campus. Any more questions?"

"Sorry. I guess grown-ups don't like snow days as much as kids do," I said.

"It just messes up everybody's schedule, Fran. Nobody catches up."

"Come to think of it, that's probably the *only* advantage of working in this tiny kitchen: I never have to get my feet wet."

"You see? Wouldn't you be foolish to rent space somewhere and give yourself more headaches?" Dad said.

"No, I wouldn't be foolish. Maybe I owe it to my career to do just that. Not to mention my growth as a fully independent human being."

"Good God, Margaret."

The phone rang, and as I went in to answer it, I could hear their voices from the kitchen. Words like *hostile, unsupportive, inconsiderate* flew around in the air like bats. I closed the door before I picked up the receiver.

"Fran? Can you believe it? A snow day already!"

"Hi, Sarah. Isn't it great? I had the weirdest experience." I told her about my dream and how surprised I was that it was really snowing when I woke up.

"You probably woke up earlier and saw the snow, then went back to sleep, and when you woke up the second time, you forgot about waking up the first time."

"You think so?"

"Definitely."

"I guess you're right," I said.

"Wanna ride our sleds in the park?"

"Sure. When do you want to go?"

"Marcie's picking me up in an hour."

I wondered if Marcie had called her, and then she had called me to make sure I came along, or if she had called Marcie first, and they had made their plans, and I was just an afterthought. I was always worrying about things like that.

"That's awfully early," I said.

Sarah sounded peeved. "Well, *we're* gonna go. If you don't want to, we can go without you."

An hour later, I was making my way down the street to Sarah's building. They hadn't shoveled the sidewalk yet, and I was stumbling along like the abominable snowman, wearing my oldest pair of jeans—the ones that were two inches too short—with long johns under them and leg warmers over them. I couldn't find my gloves, so I was wearing a pair of my mother's that were too big and an ugly color. I felt the way I used to when I was little and Mom would bundle me up in so many clothes that I could hardly walk. It was really cold, but the snow was drifting down lazily now, the fury of the early morning storm was over.

Sarah and Marcie were waiting for me inside their doorway.

"What took you so long?" Marcie said.

I just ignored her. "I think the sun's coming out!" I said to Sarah.

"I hope so," she said, sniffling.

The weather did seem to be improving. A misty glow was rising from the Hudson River as we walked toward Riverside Drive. At Eighty-third Street, the steep hill that went down into the park was our favorite for sled riding.

"You go first," Marcie ordered as we stood at the top, adjusting our hats, scarves, and gloves.

"Aren't you guys coming?" I asked.

"Of course we are. But it's getting crowded. Let's go single file," she said.

"Okay." I threw myself on my sled and took off down the hill. My first ride of the winter! I thumped along, gaining speed just as I had to swerve to a stop to avoid a couple of little kids standing near the bottom of the hill.

I brushed off the snow and started back up, but when I had gotten about halfway, Marcie and Sarah passed me going down on either side. No fair, I wanted to yell, we were supposed to go single file! Staggering to the top, out of breath, I decided to sit down and wait until the three of us could go down together. It was more fun that way.

I sat on my sled, staring out at the huge expanse of dull gray that was the Hudson River in wintertime. Suddenly, I felt a painful thud against my back. I jumped up and spun around, just in time to get a faceful of snow. Charlie Bidwell was getting ready to blast me with another one, while Timmy Shaw stood at his side, laughing like it was the funniest thing in the world.

"Charlie Bidwell, you're such a creep—" but I didn't get a chance to finish the sentence. He had good aim, I'll say that for Charlie.

Marcie and Sarah had reached the top of the hill, and when they saw what was going on, they began to pelt snow back at the guys, squealing like a couple of piglets. Charlie let out with a few more, nailing Marcie, and then Sarah. Then he and Timmy ran off along the top of the Drive, and the three of us collapsed into the snow.

"Oh my gosh," Marcie said to Sarah. "I thought I'd die!"

"You were so cool," Sarah said. "You handled it really well."

"What's going on?" I asked. "What'd you handle? You'd think you'd never had a snowball thrown at you before." They both broke into a fit of giggles. "What am I missing?"

Sarah looked at Marcie, and Marcie looked at Sarah, and then they both said, "Oh, *nothing*," in this exaggerated singsong voice.

"Don't tell me that one of you guys likes Timmy Shaw! He's a moron!" More giggling. "Sarah, I know *you* don't like him, so tell Marcie what a jerk he is."

"We know, we know, Fran. Timmy Shaw is a real jerk." Again uncontrollable laughter.

"I mean, you don't really *like* him, Marcie, do you?"

Marcie whirled around to face me. "Honestly, Fran Davies, you are so dense. Nobody likes Timmy Shaw, okay? Now will you shut up?"

The two of them settled on their sleds and got ready to go down the hill.

"Hey, wait for me!" I cried. I don't know why they even bothered to invite me along.

So, if they didn't like Timmy Shaw, why all the giggling? I usually knew who Sarah liked, and vice versa; I knew her taste pretty well, and I was sure Timmy Shaw wasn't it.

I started down after them, and as I chased their streaking sleds through the snow, the thought hit me with such fury that I almost lost control and crashed into a tree. Marcie—worse, my-used-to-be-best-friend, Sarah McAuliffe—liked the meanest boy in New York City: the cat experimenter, Charlie Bidwell. The estrangement was complete.

"Canned goods to the left, pasta and legumes to the right, miscellaneous foodstuffs in the middle."

Mrs. Hayward kept repeating the directions over and over in a high, squeaky voice as I shuffled along in back of Teresa Colón, clutching my three cans of Campbell's soup as if they were the crown jewels. Sarah, Marcie, Teresa, and I filed out of the school basement together.

"I wonder who gets all this stuff," Marcie asked.

"Poor people," Sarah said.

I had the feeling, standing between Marcie and Teresa while this conversation was going on, that Marcie didn't *believe* in poor people. They were like the tooth fairy or the Easter bunny, only not as cute.

Teresa was new in school, and I don't think she had made many friends yet, so I asked her to join us. Marcie was new, too, but it was different for her. She spoke English better than Teresa, for one thing, and Marcie, of course, had Sarah. I noticed the two of them exchanging looks as Teresa sat down.

"Yuk, watercress again!" Marcie said, rolling up her

70

sandwich and stuffing it back into her lunch bag. "My mother better realize I'm not a stupid rabbit," she said. "What's on the menu today? I've gotta buy again."

"Chili," I said. "But you eat it at your own risk."

"I love chili," Teresa said. "All kinds of chili."

I rolled my eyes at her. "You wouldn't love the kind they serve here," I said.

"She probably would," Marcie said, making a face. "I think I'll just get a couple of Yodels." She went back on the line.

I glanced uneasily over at Teresa, but she pretended not to have noticed what Marcie had said.

"The hamburgers here are the worst. I think they were made the year the school was built—when was that, 1946?" I asked Sarah. "Then they just put them in the freezer until the moment we want them, when they're popped on the grill."

"Yeah, and the chicken salad," Sarah added. "One million dollars to the person who finds a piece of chicken."

Teresa sat silently eating her sandwich.

"How was the food in your old school?" I asked her.

She shook her head. "I dunno. I always brought from home."

Marcie came back and put two Yodels, a candy bar, and a Coke on the table.

"Nutritious lunch," Sarah said.

"Are you sure you're the daughter of a dentist?" I said pointedly.

"That's why I'm here and not back in Short Hills.

Boy, would he have loved to have me stay back there so he could guard my gums!" she said, giggling.

Teresa finished eating and got up to go.

"Where ya going?" I asked.

She glanced over at Marcie. "I have to do some things before English," she said.

"You know what she has to do before English, don't you?" Marcie said as we watched Teresa make her way through the cafeteria. "Learn to speak it!" and she let out a coyote-like howl.

"That's so dumb, Marcie," I said.

"What's so dumb? That's honestly the only thing I don't like about living in the city. Kids like her. We didn't have any of them out in Short Hills."

"What d'you mean, kids like her?"

Marcie rolled her eyes. "Skip it," she said.

But I didn't want to skip it. "What are you, a bigot?"

"Fran! That's a terrible thing to say! Of course she isn't, are you, Metcalfe?"

"I wouldn't even dignify that remark with an answer."

"*See,*" Sarah said.

I looked at her. "How come you get mad at me for saying she's a bigot, but you don't get mad at her for making those cracks about Teresa? What's happened to you, Sarah?"

"Nothing's happened to me, Davies. Everybody doesn't have to like who you like, you know. Isn't your good friend Andrea Fairchild called the town snot? What's worse, a snot or a bigot?"

72

Marcie giggled. "One sounds much more *refined*," she said, fluttering her eyelashes.

"So long, you two," I said. "I just remembered I have something to do before English, too."

All I had to do was go to the bathroom, but I had to get away from them. How could Sarah have changed so much? What did she find to like in horrible Marcie Metcalfe?

Since I have piano lessons with Mrs. Barry on Tuesdays, I hurried home without waiting for Sarah and Marcie after school. But I had rushed away from them only to burst in on Mom and Connie Beck.

Marcie's mother was wearing a beige sweater, one of her long skirts, boots, and this time, a paisley shawl thrown over her shoulders. She always had something draped over her, like a bullfighter. Plus, of course, she wore the shades. I realized they were pink-tinted glasses, and she wore them all the time. They were her regular eyeglasses. Mom was wearing her basic oxford shirt and jeans. I wondered how long it would be before Mom started dressing in "earthen tones" and draping tablecloths over her shoulders.

"Darling, look at this! Isn't it yummy?" My mom was talking funny again. I dropped my books on the chair and went over to the window where Mom and C.B. were standing. Mom was holding a swatch of fabric in the sunlight. It looked like one of those sacks potatoes come in.

"It looks like one of those sacks potatoes come in," I said.

"Oh, does your daughter have a good eye, or does your daughter have a good eye!" C.B. said while Mom smiled at me.

"You mean, it's supposed to look like a potato sack?"

"Well, sweetie," Mom said, "it's supposed to represent the essence of a potato sack. What a potato sack means. You know, simplicity, roots, the home as shelter."

Connie Beck was looking at Mom through those tinted glasses and nodding approvingly, like a teacher whose pupil has memorized something perfectly.

"But where are you going to put it?" I asked.

Mom looked at C.B., and C.B. looked at Mom, and almost at the same time, they chorused, "Everywhere!"

"It will express your mom's genre perfectly, Fran. Food as nourishment for the body and the soul; that which surrounds the simplest of foods will surround your home." She spoke in a low voice, with that measured, patient tone I had noted earlier.

"You'll see, Fran," Mom said, "it's going to make this place so much warmer. It's going to wrap us in security."

I felt as if I were being wrapped in cow manure. Did Mom really believe this stuff? Maybe Dad and I could commit Mom to some nice, quiet sanatorium until the C.B. syndrome had worn off. "You're really going to decorate our apartment in potato sacks?" I asked. But they didn't answer.

"This place is going to be *you,* finally," C.B. was saying to Mom as they floated into the kitchen, their coffee cups held in front of them like scepters. "You can't camouflage yourself any longer, Margaret. It would be tragic. You have strong primitive instincts, and your home has to reflect this, or your potential is going to be strangled. Emotionally strangled."

"Mom, I have my piano lesson, so I have to run," I called into the kitchen. Then I grabbed my music book and went out the door.

Mrs. Barry's apartment was on the ground floor of Sarah's building. I had been taking lessons for two years now, and I don't think I was getting any better, even though Mrs. Barry kept saying she saw a vast improvement. When I rang the bell, I could hear her shuffling down the hallway of the small apartment. Then she looked through the keyhole and opened the door.

"Good afternoon, Francine, and how are we today?"

"Fine, Mrs. Barry," I said. Going in and closing the door, I followed the frail figure down the narrow hallway. As always, I noticed how immense the shawl-draped piano looked in the tiny living room. The only other furniture was a wing chair, a straight-backed chair, and a table between them.

As I placed my songbook on the piano, she asked, "Have we been practicing the new piece?"

"Yes, of course," I lied.

It was called "Dance of the Mad Gypsies," and it

sounded exactly the same as the last piece and the piece before that. I concentrated on reading the notes and hoped the lesson would go quickly.

I had started taking lessons because Sarah was taking lessons. That's the way it was with a lot of things: Sarah did them because I did them, or I did them because Sarah did. It was beginning to seem pretty dumb.

At the end of the lesson, Mrs. Barry liked to give me a drawing. I'm getting pretty old to get pictures of ducks and birds, but I don't know how to tell her that. She makes these drawings in two minutes flat, and the little kids really love them. Today she drew a turtle. I knew it was a turtle because she told me so. If I had had to guess, I might have said a dachshund wearing a sombrero, so I'm really glad she tipped me off.

As I left Mrs. Barry and started down the hall, the door to Marcie's apartment opened, and I could hear them giggling even before I saw Sarah come out.

"Call you later," she was saying over her shoulder to Marcie. Then she saw me and stopped.

"Hi," I said.

"Hi," she said.

I didn't know whether to stop or not, so I just kept going, as if I were hurrying home to do something really important.

"Talk to you later," I heard Marcie call, as Sarah started up the stairs.

When I came into the kitchen, Mom had scraps of paper thumbtacked all over a bulletin board she had hung on the wall.

"Are these orders for Thanksgiving dinners?" I asked.

"Not whole dinners, just special dishes. You know, people want to cook their own turkeys, but they want to jazz up the dinner a bit. I wish C.B. hadn't stayed so long. I really have to get organized."

"Can I help?"

"Thanks, Fran, but I'm past the point of made-at-home-with-loving-hands. This stuff is strictly professional."

"Well, I can help with our own Thanksgiving dinner, can't I? Remember last year, you let me make the cranberry sauce and the pumpkin pie?"

"That's right—yipes, that seems like a million years ago. This year, I'm afraid it's going to be very simple, Fran. I'll have my hands full, filling these orders."

"Oh," I said.

Steve came in and slammed the door noisily. "Any phone calls?"

"I wrote your messages down on the telephone pad. Three phone calls, Lancelot, all girls."

"Great," he said, going over and tearing the sheet off the message pad. He made his way down the hall to the bedroom.

"Mom, I think Steve's getting real conceited. He thinks he's the coolest thing in jeans."

"He's got a right to be conceited, Fran. The girls are all crazy about him. Now, why don't you go and start your homework so you get to bed at a decent hour?" she said, making a shooing motion with her hand.

77

It took me less than an hour to do my homework, and dinner wasn't ready yet, so I took out a piece of my new stationery.

Dear Andrea,

I felt so bad when I got your letter saying that you couldn't come for a visit. But I know that you feel bad, too, so that makes me feel better. Does that make any sense?

Can you believe that it's almost Thanksgiving already? Did you have as much snow as we did? We went sledding every day that week. Do you get to see Brenda or her gang at all? If you do, say hello for me.

I found out that Sarah likes the most horrible boy in our whole school. I think it's just because he's the only boy we know who's growing. *I hope I never get that desperate. I'm sure you'd hate him like I do.*

Well, nothing else is new here. I just wanted to say hi, so you wouldn't forget me.

Love from your friend,
Fran

When I went to bed, Mom was still working in the kitchen. She was being awfully noisy. Maybe she was mad about something again.

I didn't go to sleep right away. I lay awake for a long time thinking about how different things were from the way I thought they'd be when I first invited Andrea for a visit. I had wanted her to see how happy my family was (even though we didn't live in a mansion), and I had wanted her to meet my best friend, Sarah McAuliffe. Now I wasn't sure I had a best friend named Sarah McAuliffe, and things were so different with our family. These days, Mom was either acting weird with Connie Beck or banging pans around angrily in the middle of the night. As I lay there listening to the clatter, I tried to figure out which I hated more. I drifted off to sleep before I could decide.

10
○

I don't just get caught up in the holiday spirit, I get kidnapped by it. I buy these magazines with fantastic pictures on the front and cover blurbs that promise *Christmas presents to delight and dazzle from scraps you'd throw away!* I have a whole shoe box filled with scraps that never managed to delight and dazzle. But I never learn. Every year it's the same thing: When we flip the calendar to December, my pulse starts to race, and I get this tingling in my toes that gradually works its way up through my whole body. Pretty soon, I'm humming "Jingle Bells" under my breath. I drive people crazy.

This year I had planned to make a centerpiece of Santa, a sled, and eight reindeer out of a roll of red foil, some brown paper bags from D'Agostino's, and thirty cents' worth of trim. I also planned to make a patchwork potholder for Mom, a patchwork book cover for Dad, a personalized scrapbook for Steve, and a tiny velvet jewelry box for Sarah. Maybe, just maybe, I'd buy something for Marcie. I had gotten these ideas from the December issue of *Woman's World* magazine. They also had a gorgeous layout of Christmas-tree ornaments you could make from—you guessed it—

"scraps you'd throw away." I took the magazine into the kitchen.

"Look, Mom, aren't these gorgeous?" I asked, showing her the spread.

She threw a quick glance over her glasses, which were perched precariously on the end of her nose.

"Mmm . . . pretty," she mumbled. "But you're not going to try to make them, are you?" she said, looking at me worriedly as she flipped a pot of pasta into a colander in the sink.

"Well, yeah, I thought I would."

"Oh, Fran, things are so hectic this year. Tell you what, why don't we just buy some nice ornaments? I'll give you extra money, how's that?"

"But I want to *make* stuff. Anyway, you don't have to help me," I said, and I grabbed my coat and headed out the door.

She didn't even ask me where I was going. That's one good thing about having a working mother: It sure cuts down on the nagging.

I rang Sarah's doorbell and waited. What if Marcie was in there with her? Maybe this was a dumb idea. I was about to turn and run, when I heard Sarah say, "I'll call you back, Metcalfe. Somebody's at the door."

I heard the click of the peephole, and then Sarah swung the door open. "Hi," she said, just like always. What did I expect, that she'd greet me at the door with a blast of machine-gun fire?

She stepped aside, and I went in. I was holding the magazine down at my side like a concealed weapon. After we had sat down in the living room, I found the

81

page with the multicolored velvet balls and showed it to her.

"Ooh," she said, in a way that let me know she really thought they were neat. "Are you going to make these?" She was looking at me with awe and admiration.

I nodded. "I'm going to try."

"They look pretty complicated. "Don't you need a lot of stuff?"

"Not really. That's what I like about it. It says you can make them from scraps you'd ordinarily just throw away." I took the magazine and found the page that listed the supplies. She read intently, wrinkling her forehead over some of the items.

"Do you have one yard each of red, green, silver, purple, and turquoise velvet?"

I shook my head.

"How about sixteen inches of French lace?"

"Nope."

"Seed pearls? Sequins?"

"Not at the moment."

"How about bejeweled stickpins?"

I grabbed the magazine back. "All right, all right, so I'll need to get a few things."

"That's what they call scraps you'd throw away?"

"I guess if you were Princess Diana, you would," I said, giggling.

"You want to do them together?"

"I was hoping you'd want to."

"Remember the gingerbread house we made when we were little?"

I let out a shriek. "The kitchen! It looked like a volcano had erupted all over the walls!"

"Your mom was so great. She didn't even yell at us."

"Yeah. I think those days are gone forever."

"What d'you mean?"

"Oh, nothing."

"Come on, what's the matter? You seem so grumpy lately. You having trouble with your mom?"

"I haven't been grumpy," I snapped. "She's just, I don't know, getting very liberated. Marcie's mother is over all the time, and you know how she is."

"Yeah, she's kind of weird. But you shouldn't complain. I wish my mom would go to work. She watches everything I do. It's like having a parole officer."

"That's one good thing. I could dye my hair orange, and she wouldn't notice it for a month. But it's kind of a lonely feeling."

"Oh, I hate that. It was pretty lonely around here last summer when you went away, before Metcalfe moved in."

I wanted to say something about Marcie, but I hesitated. Sarah and I were talking the way we used to, and I didn't want to spoil it. She went over and started to rummage in a drawer where her mother keeps her sewing things. Maybe if I worded it right . . .

"So I guess you didn't miss me at all after Marcie moved in, huh?" I hoped it sounded very casual.

She stared at me. "I never said that. What are you trying to do, Davies, start a fight?"

I could feel myself flush. "Don't call me Davies."

"Why not?" she said, sounding really annoyed, as if I was the one who was being peculiar. "It's your name, isn't it?"

"Fran's my name. You never used to call me Davies. So why do you do it now?"

"Because it's cool. We started doing it this summer, when you were away."

"Sarah, you keep saying 'when you were away,' as if it was something I did to you. I didn't exactly have a blast, you know."

"You could have fooled me."

"What does that mean?"

"Look, you lived in a mansion, didn't you? And you went to a country club? And you went horseback riding? And you didn't even tell me where you were going! So don't expect me to feel sorry for you."

I stared at Sarah. She was hurling accusations at me for all the things I did with Andrea. Things that I wrote her about. She was mad at me for leaving for the whole summer. But that was silly! I didn't want to continue with this conversation because I *had* lied to Sarah, and I still felt guilty about it.

"I shouldn't have told you the truth at all," I said.

"You didn't have to."

I looked at her. "What's that supposed to mean?"

"I knew all along."

"You're lying!"

"Look who's calling who a liar!"

"How could you know?"

"Your mom told my mom, before you left."

"Oh." I had been afraid of that. "But you never said anything!"

"What was I going to say? But I was really hurt, Fran. If you wanted to lie to everybody else in school, okay. I wouldn't have given you away. But you don't lie to your best friend. So I figured you didn't consider me your best friend anymore."

"Sarah—"

"Maybe Andrea Fairchild is your best friend now."

"I don't even see Andrea Fairchild. I'll probably never see her again. It's you and Marcie who are best friends."

"Maybe we are."

It was as if she had hit me. Neither of us said anything for a moment. Then she added, "At least she doesn't lie to me. You lied to me, Fran. Not just before you left, but the whole summer. Every time you wrote to me, you lied."

"It's okay, Sarah. It's a free country," I said. "You're free to be best friends with whomever you like." I was about to make some kind of dramatic exit, like maybe through the third-floor window, when the phone rang.

"Hi, Metcalfe. No, it was only Davies." I flinched. "Hey, that's a neat idea. Let me ask her if she wants to." She put her hand over the phone. "Metcalfe wants the three of us to go Christmas shopping together on Saturday. You want to?"

I shrugged my shoulders to show how independent I was, and how I really didn't care whether they included me in things or not. Then I nodded my head quickly before they could take back the invitation.

"Yeah, she wants to. Let's go down Broadway. Yeah, that's good. Okay. See you tomorrow."

I picked up the magazine and started toward the door.

"It's a good thing Metcalfe's so organized. I haven't even *begun* my shopping yet, have you?" she asked.

I shook my head. "I'm going to make most of my presents."

"Oh. Well, you're more ambitious than I am. See you tomorrow," she said breezily.

"Right," I said. "So long."

After the apartment door closed, as I waited for the elevator, I realized we hadn't said anything more about making the tree ornaments together. Maybe I'd just buy some, after all.

11

There wasn't room on the sidewalk for the three of us to walk together, so I trailed behind—almost, but not quite, managing to stay in the middle and keep up with the conversation.

"You wanna start here and work our way down, or start downtown and work our way up?" Sarah asked.

We had stopped for a light at the corner of Eighty-third and West End Avenue, and they turned and looked at me. Marcie was wearing a shocking pink turtleneck under a fuchsia jacket. The little Christmas balls that dangled from her ears swayed back and forth to the rhythm of her gum chewing. I shrugged my shoulders. "Maybe we should start downtown, then we'll be coming closer to home as we go along." Marcie made a face like that was a really dumb idea. "I don't care," I said in exasperation. "You asked my opinion, you know," I said to Sarah.

"Okay, okay, Davies, take it easy. We'll go down to Carter's," she said as the light changed and they crossed the street.

"Wait up!" I called, hurrying after them. Under her Jordache jeans, Marcie was wearing high-heeled boots.

How could she walk so fast? As they turned to wait for me, I was struck again by the wild colors in her outfit. She sure didn't dress like her mother.

By the time we got to Carter's, I was really cold. I had worn gloves, so my hands were okay, but I hadn't worn a hat, of course, so my ears were freezing.

Carter's was something like Woolworth's, only fancier. It had everything from pots and pans and dishes to toys and stationery. Sarah wanted to get a stuffed animal for Benjamin, so we went to the toy counter first.

"Look at this!" Sarah cried, picking up a really cute stuffed panda. "Isn't he adorable? Oh, forget it," she said, dropping him quickly when she looked at the price tag.

"Here's one like it, only smaller," I said.

"Naah, it doesn't have the same face. See, its eyes are too close together, so it has kind of a dumb look."

"Perfect for Benjamin," Marcie quipped.

"Marcie!"

But Sarah only laughed. "Don't worry, Davies, Metcalfe's just being honest. I know Benjamin's dopey-looking."

"But he's only three years old," I protested. "I think he's cute."

"I didn't say he wasn't cute," Marcie said, laughing. "I think he's very cute. Dumb-looking, but cute."

Sarah had moved down to some stuffed reindeer that had bells on their antlers and red ribbons around their necks. "What do you think of these?" she asked.

I didn't know whether she was asking Marcie or me,

but before I had a chance to answer, Marcie said, "Perfect."

Sarah tucked it under her arm. "One down, four to go."

"What are you getting your mom?" I asked her.

"I dunno yet. What're you getting yours?"

"I'm making her a potholder," I said. I thought I heard Marcie snickering behind me. "But, of course," I added quickly, hating myself, "I'm going to buy her something, too. Maybe something for the kitchen, some gadget she doesn't have."

"That's a good idea, and it'll go with the potholder. Should I get my mom something like that?" Sarah asked.

"Your mom would probably love something like that," Marcie said. "No offense, McAuliffe, but my mom says your mom is a real 'cookie baker.'"

Sarah laughed. "That's my mom!"

"That's one of the things my mom hated about New Jersey. She said she was surrounded by 'cookie bakers.'"

"Actually, my mom's more of a cookie baker than Sarah's," I said. "I mean, she's a *professional* cookie baker."

"Oh Fran, that's just an expression. No, my mom says your mom's a person who's got her own identity, almost. She thinks your mom's neat." I wasn't sure how she expected me to react to this outpouring of praise, but if she was waiting for me to swoon with joy, she was going to have a long wait. I didn't say anything, and she went on. "Anyway, I'll probably get my mother something in Lulu's. She really likes their stuff."

Lulu's was a boutique that looked and smelled like an opium den. Not that I've ever been in an opium den, of course. But you know what they're supposed to be like. In *Raiders of the Lost Ark,* remember? Very exotic and dangerous and smelly. Personally, I think the stuff that they sell in Lulu's looks kind of dirty.

Sarah said, "Maybe I'll get my mom something there, too. Something unusual. Last Mother's Day, my dad got her a blender, and I don't think she was out of her mind over it."

I bought my mother a little gadget that slices hardboiled eggs. She had one just like it, but she broke it last week, so I figured she could use a replacement. I also bought some Christmas cards and wrapping paper.

As I stood in line to pay, I heard loud squeals behind me, punctuated by the unmistakable horselaugh of Charlie Bidwell. Charlie had obviously done something horrible to Sarah, and they were screaming and laughing and in general making utter fools of themselves. I turned and stared straight ahead at the cashier, as if I didn't know any of them.

"Charlie, give me my scarf!" Sarah was yelling. "I'm going to freeze going home, and it'll be *your* fault." I felt something land on my shoulder, and I grabbed at the blue plaid scarf as it threatened to slide off onto the dusty floor.

"It looks better on Fran. She should wear it," he said, ambling out the door after his friends.

Sarah came up to me, giggling, and took the scarf.

"He is so weird," she said. She was extremely out of breath considering all she'd been doing was bantering with a gawky, pimply-faced boy who likes to throw kittens out of windows. She tied the scarf around her neck, and we pushed our way out of Carter's and headed uptown.

We hit McGrory's, where I bought Steve a genuine imitation-leather scrapbook for all his football clippings. I had started to make him one, but it looked so pathetic that I threw it in the garbage. At Dayton's, Sarah and I bought our fathers the same thing: a navy blue tie, with little green Christmas trees on it.

"That's pretty dumb, you know," Marcie said, as we took the ties up to the cash register. "They'll only be able to wear them one day."

I glanced over at Sarah, but she didn't seem to be listening as she counted out some change for the cashier. It must be wonderful to have the courage of your convictions, like Sarah.

"I figure my dad can wear it all through the holidays," she answered, finally.

"And not only this year, but *every* year," I added, suddenly feeling secure about my purchase. I stepped up after Sarah was finished and paid for my tie, too. "What are you getting for your father?" I asked Marcie, but she walked away as if she hadn't heard me.

"Let's hurry up, or Lulu's will be closed before we get there," she said.

Compared to the stores we'd just left, Lulu's was

practically empty. As maybe you've guessed, it wasn't exactly a Santa's workshop kind of place. I browsed around for a few minutes while Sarah and Marcie pored over a counter heaped with different colored bracelets, necklaces, and earrings. When I joined them, Marcie had already selected a necklace for her mother that looked like a piece of rope knotted with small brown beads. Then she and Sarah began trying on small gold bracelets studded with multicolored stones. Sarah turned to me.

"These are called friendship bracelets. They're from somewhere in the Orient. Where'd she say?" she asked Marcie.

"I'm not sure. Burma, I think. They're pretty, aren't they?" Marcie said, holding her wrist out for me to admire.

I looked closely at the stones and the little filigree chain. I had to admit it was pretty. I nodded.

"Hey," Marcie said, giving a little jump, "why don't we give these to each other as Christmas presents? Then we're sure to like what we get!" She was looking at Sarah as she spoke. Sarah looked over at me and hesitated.

"They *are* pretty," she said. I held my breath. "What do you think, Fran?"

I let out my breath slowly. At least I had been consulted. I thought of the little velvet jewelry box I had started making for Sarah. I looked at the bracelet on Marcie's arm.

"It *is* nice," I said. "If you want to, Sarah," I said, "I don't care."

Sarah touched the bracelet in her hand, examining it closely.

"Come on, let's! I mean, they're *friendship* bracelets, aren't they?" Marcie persisted.

Sarah looked at me directly, and for a split second I think she felt bad. I think she knew what I knew, that this was the end of a special friendship between us.

"Okay," she said then. "Let's get them."

"They'll be our special link. Friends forever!" Marcie cried gleefully. We chose three, and as the salesgirl gift wrapped the small boxes, she rattled on. "Mine'll be from you and Fran, Sarah's will be from Fran and me, and Fran's will be from Sarah and me." She seemed so happy; for a second, I was almost glad for her.

We each paid for one and left Lulu's with a tiny gift-wrapped package, not to be opened until Christmas. As we walked home, I decided I would finish making the jewelry box for Sarah anyway.

We rounded the corner of Eighty-third Street just as it began to get dark and a few small snowflakes started to fall. We had to step around a huge mound of Christmas trees piled on the sidewalk. It was a perfect Christmas setting, and I should have been filled with Christmas spirit, but I wasn't. Everything was so different this year. Merriweather had changed everything.

"That you, Fran?" my mother said as I entered the apartment. She poked her head out the kitchen doorway. "Hurry up. You've got a phone call."

"Who is it?" I asked, dropping my packages on the

93

hall table and taking the phone she held out to me from the wall in the kitchen. I stripped off my gloves as I said "Hello?"

"Fran? Hi, it's me, Andrea."

"Andrea?" I said hesitantly into the telephone, as if it were a strange new instrument I had never used before.

"Yeah! How *are* you?"

"Fine. How are *you?*"

"Great! Listen, you know how you sent me a letter asking me to come for a visit?"

"Yeah."

"Well, I can come!"

"You can? That's terrific! *When?*"

"Richard and Maggie are going to Switzerland skiing after Christmas, and Bertha can't be here for four days, so all of a sudden, New York doesn't seem so dangerous!"

"You mean your stepfather definitely said you could come and stay with us?"

"That's right! Are you glad?"

"Oh, Andrea, you don't know how glad! When will you be here?"

"The twenty-eighth. And I can stay until the first—if that's all right."

"Of course it is! You can spend New Year's Eve with us!"

"Yeah. Won't that be great?"

"You bet. Are you coming on the train?"

"Yeah. Richard is going to call your folks and check everything out."

"We'll meet you at Grand Central."

"New York for the holidays. Doesn't it sound exciting? By the way, your cousin invited me to her birthday party."

"Did you go?"

"I sure did. I got Maggie to let me, and it was fun. Her friend Eva Marie is having a party over the holidays, but I guess I'll have to turn that one down—*if* I'm invited."

"I'm sure you will be."

"Well, I'll write to you, okay?"

"And then we can make our plans. We'll have a blast, Andrea."

I waited a second to hear her hang up, then I hung up, too.

When I turned around, Mom was standing in the kitchen doorway.

"I guess you heard," I said.

"Yes, I did," she said. "When is she coming?"

"Three days after Christmas. And she can stay until New Year's Day."

My mother sighed and went back into the kitchen. I followed her.

"What's the matter now?"

"Nothing's the matter, Fran," she said, not looking at me but punching a piece of dough awfully hard.

"Don't you want Andrea to come?"

"I don't mind her coming, hon. It's just the timing. Things are going to be so hectic then. New Year's Eve . . . I *told* you about the Sheffield party."

"She won't get in the way," I said quietly.

95

Mom let out a sigh and came over and gave me a hug. "I know she won't, Fran. I'm glad she's coming; it'll be nice for you. And after all, *I* was the one responsible for you two becoming friends in the first place! Now you'll have to buy her a present, won't you?"

"That's right!" I said.

I had another good friend to buy a present for. Maybe not a best friend, yet, but you never know. As I took the packages into my room, I could feel my pulse begin to race, and I got this tingling in my toes that gradually worked its way up through my whole body.

By suppertime, I was humming "Jingle Bells."

12

"Fran, hurry up. Andrea's train gets in at 9:05. You don't want to be late."

My father stood near the front door, impatiently fiddling with a woolen scarf Mom had given him for Christmas.

"I'm ready!" I cried, giving my room one last look. I had spent two whole days cleaning it, and I wanted to make sure everything was perfect. Luckily, Dad had thrown a fit when he heard some of C.B.'s decorating ideas. It was a whopper of an argument, but the sane group won. I really didn't want my mother to be emotionally strangled, but if it came to that or living in a potato field, I guess Mom was going to have to take her chances.

Dad glanced at his watch again. "She'd better not have too much stuff with her, or we'll never get on the bus at this hour."

"Why don't you take a cab, Jim? It would be much nicer than trying to squeeze on one of those crowded buses at rush hour. Andrea's not used to that."

"That's a great idea, Mom!"

"That's not a great idea, Fran. Are we going to spend the whole week trying to impress Andrea Fairchild? Maybe we should let her see how the other half lives."

"Jim, don't be nasty. I only meant that it would be faster, save you time. Be nice, for Fran's sake."

They glared at each other for a minute, and then my father opened the door, and we left. He hardly spoke all the way down to Grand Central station.

Knowing that Andrea was coming had kept my spirits up, but this was surely a strange holiday for our family. The piles of presents under the tree were higher than last year, but everybody's spirits were lower. Mom kept complaining about how busy she was, and Dad kept complaining about Mom's complaining.

To top it off, two weeks ago Steve announced that Christmas was nothing but commercial hogwash and he didn't intend to celebrate it this year. Then he proceeded to do a wonderful imitation of Scrooge. He wouldn't wrap a present or even help to trim the tree. Christmas morning he thawed long enough to give me a wallet, and I think he really liked the scrapbook I gave him, but it was a close call.

I had shopped carefully for Andrea's present and finally settled on a pretty yellow picture frame. I was going to put my picture in it, but I decided to wait until she asked me for one.

We arrived at Grand Central with only five minutes to spare and hurried over to check which track Andrea's train would be arriving on.

"Number twenty-eight," I said, scanning the big schedule posted above the ticket windows.

We got to the gate just as the conductor opened it. I looked down and saw the big silver train shrieking its arrival as it slid to a stop. In a moment, hordes of people began pouring out of its doors. They all melted together as they scurried up the ramp like mice, but as they reached the top, they took on real shapes and sizes. They became men and women, young and old, fat and skinny. But the more people I saw, the more confusing it was. I couldn't see Andrea anywhere. I scanned the faces hurriedly as the commuters came through the gates and disappeared into the anonymous crowds behind us. Then suddenly, she was there.

"Andrea!" I screamed, so loudly that several people turned around. She looked over and waved. When she reached us, she dropped her suitcase, and we gave each other a quick hug. Then she looked up at my father, held out her hand, and said, "Hello, Mr. Davies. It's nice to see you again." I had almost forgotten about Andrea's manners.

"Hello, Andrea," he said, shaking hands. "How've you been?"

"Fine, thank you."

Dad picked up the suitcase—I was glad to see that there was only one—and began to navigate our way out of the crowds. As we made our way back up to

Forty-second Street, I remembered how much Andrea had admired my father. Her dad had been a teacher, too, but now she hardly ever saw him. In his place, she had Richard Fairchild, who wore a paisley scarf around his neck.

"Gosh, it's good to see you again," I said.

"It's good to see you, too."

Dad had stopped on the side of the street where the cabs line up, and my heart gave a little leap as he stepped to the curb and, opening a cab door, motioned us to get in.

I looked over at Andrea as we settled back and the cab drove away from the curb. She was wearing tweed slacks and a lavender turtleneck with a mauve down jacket over it. As always, she looked splendid. Or, as I had thought the first time I met her, like an ad for Lord & Taylor. Which reminded me . . .

"Have you ever seen the Lord & Taylor windows during the holidays?" I asked.

"I think I did once, a few years ago, when we first moved East. Are those the windows where they have scenes with little people and animals, and everything moves around?"

"That's it. Lots of stores have fancy windows at this time of year, but Lord & Taylor's have always been my favorite. I always feel like I'm looking into the biggest dollhouse in the world. They have tiny chandeliers, and all the little furniture is so neat. We can go there one day, if you'd like to," I said finally, which was my main point all along.

100

"I'd like that," she said.

Andrea settled back in the cab and looked out at the streets going by with such a look of excitement on her face that I felt it, too. Everything was going to be fine, now that Andrea had come.

The taxi dropped us off in front of the apartment building and then hurried my father off to his school, where he had some work to catch up on.

"Is this where you live?" Andrea asked as I held the heavy glass door for her to go through. I was suddenly conscious of the loud squeaking sound the door had always made.

"No," I said, "I just thought you'd like a tour of New York City buildings."

"Okay, okay, so it was a dumb question."

We walked through the narrow lobby. I scrutinized everything: the notice up on the wall about an 83rd Street Block Association meeting, the musty old couch with its table and rickety lamp, the two unused planters on either side of the three steps leading up to the tiny elevator. I tried to see it through Andrea's eyes.

"This is nice," she said.

"I don't usually wait for the elevator, but since you have the suitcase, we might as well take it," I said, stepping aside to let her get in first.

When I knocked at our door, nobody answered, so I used my key.

"My mother should be here. She said she wouldn't be going out till later on."

There was a note on the refrigerator door.

Fran,

Sorry I won't be there to welcome Andrea, but I had a whipped-cream emergency! Be home about four. Have fun!

Love,
Mom

"Did I tell you that my mother has her own catering business now?" I said.

"That's nice," Andrea said, looking around at everything in the living room and the dinette.

"Come on, I'll show you my room."

Andrea followed me down the hall and dropped her suitcase in my doorway. She stood appraising her surroundings for a moment, just as she had outside.

"This is really *neat,*" she said finally, in a way that made me know she really meant it.

"It's pretty plain compared to your place."

She looked at me for a moment, and I remembered how little she cared for the house in Merriweather with its fancy bedroom, and how she kept all the plain things from "before" up in the attic. We didn't say any more about it, but I felt it: Our home reminded Andrea of her life before the divorce.

My brother's door opened, and he came out into the hall in his pajamas, his hair sprayed out around his head like a rock star's.

"Could you keep it down out here? I'm trying to sleep. What time is it, anyway?"

I looked over at Andrea and rolled my eyes.

"You remember my brother, don't you, Andrea—the *gallant,* the *charming,* Steve Davies?"

Andrea giggled and said, "Hi, Steve."

Steve gave me a dirty look, but he said hi to Andrea before he made his way down the hall to the bathroom.

"He's not always like that," I said. "Sometimes he's in a *bad* mood."

She laughed, and I settled myself on the bed to watch her unpack. I had cleared out one of my drawers for her, shoveling all my summer stuff into a shopping bag in the closet.

"So what do you want to do this week?" I began.

She shrugged her shoulders. "I don't care. I just love being here, Fran, honest. We don't have to do anything special."

"We can go ice skating at Rockefeller Center. Would you like that? You *do* ice skate, don't you?"

She nodded, and I realized what a stupid question that was. Andrea did *everything* well. It was really amazing that I liked her anyway.

We shoved her suitcase under the bed and went into the kitchen to get something to eat. But when I opened the refrigerator, everything was in labeled containers. There was almost nothing to eat that was unwrapped, except a stick of butter and six eggs.

"Andrea, you ever hear the saying about the shoemaker's child, how he goes barefoot?"

She smiled. "That's okay," she said.

"I could make you a burned omelet. That's the only kind I'm really good at making."

"No, thank you! Really, I'm not hungry. So, tell me, what's new with you?"

I shrugged my shoulders. "Nothing very exciting."

"Did I tell you that I went to Brenda's party?"

"You mentioned it. How was it?"

"It was fun. I didn't know all the kids, but I knew some of them. The Caulfield twins are so pretty. Have you ever met them?"

I shook my head. "What about Eva Marie Schwartzkopf? Did you get invited to her party?"

"Yes," she said, obviously delighted. "But I'm afraid I had to turn it down. It was today, as a matter of fact. I'm sure they'll miss me!" she said, rolling her eyes.

"I'm sure they will, too. They *really* will," I said earnestly.

"How's your friend Sarah?"

"Oh, she's fine. She's dying to meet you."

As if on cue, the telephone rang. "I bet that's her," I said, getting up to answer it.

I was right, and Sarah didn't need to be coaxed to come over and meet Andrea.

"She's on her way," I said, coming back into the kitchen.

"It must be nice having a friend like that. I mean one that you've known for such a long time, a real best friend."

I felt a little twinge when she said it, but I just nodded agreement. "Yeah," I said. Then, "Oh, I almost forgot!" I went over and extracted the small present still lying under the tree. "I want to give you this before anyone gets here," I said, handing it to her.

"Oh, thank you," she said. Then she jumped up and went over to her shoulder bag, which had been lying on the hall table. She handed me a really tiny box. "I hope you like it."

Swiftly and silently, we each tore the wrappings off our gifts.

"Oh, Fran, I love it," she squealed. "Now you have to give me a picture of yourself that I can put in it!"

"Okay," I said, trying not to show how pleased I was that she had asked. "I have extra copies of my school picture you can have."

I unwrapped my box, and as I had been hoping, there was a ring inside. It was a gold knot with a dark red stone. "It's beautiful," I said, slipping it on my finger.

"I'm so glad it fits! I didn't think of that until after I had bought it. It's supposed to be a ruby, but it's not, of course," she said. The doorbell rang then, and we scooped up the wrapping paper and ribbon before I went to answer it.

When I opened the door, Sarah was standing there with you-know-who at her elbow.

"Come on in," I said.

They followed me down the hall to the kitchen.

"Sarah, this is Andrea. Andrea, this is Sarah." I didn't even want to introduce Marcie, but after a pause, I said, "And this is Marcie Metcalfe."

There were hi's all around, and then everybody stood there in an awkward silence.

"Did you have a nice trip?" Marcie said finally to Andrea.

"Oh, sure," Andrea said, looking a little puzzled. "It's only forty minutes on the train."

"Oh," she said. Then she looked over at me and asked, "Did you have a nice Christmas?" There was something different about her, but I couldn't figure out what it was. She seemed, for the first time, a little strained, a little unsure of herself.

I nodded. "Fine. How about you?"

She gave a tight little smile. "Oh, great."

"How was your holiday, Andrea?" Sarah asked.

"Okay, I guess. Kind of hectic. Maggie and Richard had this trip coming up, so it was a mad scene."

When Andrea called her parents Maggie and Richard, I noticed Marcie and Sarah exchanging looks.

"So how'd your mom like her present?" Marcie asked. Whatever had been bothering her seemed to have passed, and unfortunately she was her old self again.

"The potholder? She really liked it. I think it turned out pretty good. You want to see it?"

"Not the potholder! The *sign.* The present my mother gave your mother? I see she's got it up."

Marcie looked at the spot over the sink where my mother had hung the ghastly sign C.B. had given her when she stopped by for some eggnog on Christmas Eve. It was made out of bread dough, baked and shellacked (so it was *brown*), and it said THE AWAKENED COOKIE BAKER. Suddenly everyone was staring up at it.

"She liked it," was all I said.

"My mom thinks your mom should call her business that. Wouldn't that be a cute name? Especially if she sets up in the Village. They all have crazy names down there."

"I thought you were going to visit your father," I heard myself blurt out.

"Oh, it sort of fell through. But I still might, for a few days. It all depends," she said, like it wasn't important at all. Then she looked at Andrea. "How often do you see your dad?" she asked.

If I had been chewing gum, I would have swallowed it.

"Marcie!"

Andrea looked at me quickly. "That's all right, Fran, I don't care. I don't get to see him very often," she said to Marcie. "He's remarried, and they live in California."

"Don't you go there for any of the holidays, even?" she persisted.

"Well, actually, I spent last Christmas with them, and I was supposed to spend this Christmas, but her son, who lives with *his* father, was coming, and they don't have very much room. So now the plan is, I'm going out there for spring vacation."

"That'll be nice," Marcie said. "The weather in California's supposed to be terrific."

"It is. And they have a really cute place. Like a garden apartment. Not very big, but kind of Spanish-looking, you know what I mean?"

I looked over at Sarah and raised my eyebrows. She must have gotten the message, because suddenly she said, "So what are you two doing this week?"

"I thought maybe we'd go ice skating tomorrow," I said. "And see the tree at Rockefeller Center. Do you want to come?" Sarah and I had always done that together.

"Sure," she said. Then she turned to Marcie. "Can you?"

Marcie hesitated. "Probably. Unless I go to New Jersey."

"Well, I gotta go now," Sarah said. "Nice meeting you, Andrea."

"See you tomorrow," I said.

"Right."

"So how do you like Sarah?" I asked Andrea, when I had closed the door.

"She seems really nice," she said.

"And how do you like our dear friend, Marcie Metcalfe?" I asked, making a face.

"She's nice, too."

"Oh, come on, Andrea, tell the truth. Have you ever met anyone so repulsive in your whole life?"

Andrea stared at me. "She's not that bad, Fran. Honest, I kind of liked her."

"You've got to be joking."

"No, I'm not. Why?"

"Oh, nothing," I said, deciding not to pursue the

108

subject. "Why don't we hit Burger King for lunch, and then I'll show you around the neighborhood."

"That sounds great."

So that's what we did, and I'm happy to report that a certain person's name was completely absent from our conversation for the rest of the day. In fact, if it hadn't been for Charlie Bidwell sitting right behind us at Burger King, the day would have been pretty near perfect.

Even though I see the tree every single year, each time I do, I get a little shiver of excitement at the first glimpse of it. We came around the corner into Rockefeller Center, and there it was, majestic as always, thousands and thousands of colored bulbs swaying back and forth in the gusty wind that blew through the plaza.

I turned and looked at Andrea, who was standing with her head tilted back and her mouth hanging open. She had an expression on her face like the little boy in *E.T.* "You've been here before, haven't you?" I asked.

She nodded. "Once, and I've always wanted to come back."

"I've come here lots of times," Marcie said. "Every year, in from New Jersey to see the tree. It sure is a lot more convenient this year, I gotta admit that."

We got in line to go ice skating. Even though it was only ten o'clock, there was already a long line of people waiting for their turn on the rink. I had an old pair of ice skates that fit Andrea, so we didn't have to rent a pair. But waiting was a bore. Even though the sun

110

was shining, it was icy cold, with the wind blowing tiny flakes of leftover snow into our faces. I had worn the new angora muffler I had gotten for Christmas, and I wrapped it around my face to keep warm. Each of us had worn our friendship bracelet, too, but they weren't even visible under all the clothes we were wearing.

We inched forward in line. "Isn't it neat how our mothers have become such good friends?" Marcie said, looking directly at me.

I didn't know what to say. "Oh, yeah," I said finally.

"She says your mom is an artist, only her medium is *food*. Isn't that funny? I heard them the other day, and they were so cute. They were gabbing and making plans. They're kind of like two ex-cons let out of prison at the same time."

I flushed. "My mom hasn't been in prison. She's always been very happy—"

"Isn't that Goldie Hawn over there?" Andrea interrupted.

We all turned to stare in the direction she was pointing.

"Where?" I asked.

"There, the woman with all the crazy blonde hair, in the green poncho and the sunglasses."

"That's not Goldie Hawn," Sarah said. "Goldie Hawn has a terrific figure. That woman's a blimp."

Andrea shrugged her shoulders and laughed. "Sorry. I always imagine that New York is swarming with celebrities."

"Her face does look a lot like Goldie Hawn's," Sarah said, and I nodded.

I had the feeling that Andrea had just said that to get the conversation away from Mom and Connie Beck. Andrea was so sensitive. I hadn't said anything about it to her yet, but I felt as if she saw right through me and understood. The way Sarah used to.

After about forty-five minutes, we got on the rink. By that time, it was hard to get my skates on because my fingers were so cold. When we started to skate, I watched Andrea to see if she'd start doing leaps and turns and figure eights, which would mean *I'd have to kill her.* But she just skated nice and easy, like the rest of us. There was no stopping to talk, or to adjust hats or gloves, because the rink was so crowded it was like being on a merry-go-round. We pulled over to the side after a while and watched some of the show-offs who always come to skate at Rockefeller Center. There were a couple of skaters who practically did somersaults on the ice, and there was a cute old man in a little red woolen cap who skated around and around, with his hands clasped behind his back, like the skaters in the Currier & Ives prints. There was also a little girl in a green velvet outfit. She was carrying a white fur muff, and she looked adorable. She also looked like a very good skater for such a little kid.

We started skating again, but after a few minutes, Marcie called back to us, "I want some hot chocolate!"

"You'll have to wait. If we leave now, we'll never get back on," I said, "so it's really not worth it." I yelled over to Andrea, "Once we get the skates off, we'd have to get back on that line again."

It was really crowded now. I think Andrea began to relax, because she did a few twirls on the ice that she hadn't attempted before. I could tell that Marcie and Sarah were impressed. So was I. After a while, we pulled over to the side again.

"Wanna quit and go get something?" Sarah asked, her breath coming out in white puffs as she spoke.

I looked over at Andrea. "Okay," we agreed.

After we'd climbed the stairs from the rink, Andrea and I stood leaning on the wall for a moment watching the skaters.

"Come on, I'm starved," Marcie said. "Let's get some lunch!"

"I bet we won't get in anywhere," I said. "It's the middle of the lunch hour."

We looked in two burger places that were too crowded, but at the third one, the last people in line were seated just as we came in. Marcie gave a shout.

"Hey, look over there! Those people are getting up!" We hurried over and practically threw our bodies across the table, as if daring anyone to say the booth wasn't ours. "Whew, that was lucky. If I had to stand in one more line, I think I'd die," she said.

We took off our jackets and gloves and scarves, rubbing our hands to get them warm again. When the waitress appeared, we all ordered cheeseburgers. Sarah and Andrea ordered Cokes, and Marcie and I ordered hot chocolate.

I watched Andrea as she settled herself in the booth. There was something so perfect about the way she did things. She was so graceful. Her elbows and wrists never got in each other's way, like mine do. She took off her hat, and her hair still looked terrific; she just gave it a little flip, and it settled down just like that.

Marcie whipped her hat off and then took her brush out of her pocket and started to brush her hair. I didn't say anything, but I think that is the *grossest* thing to do. My dad absolutely freaks out if he sees somebody doing that around food, and I have to say that I agree with him. Andrea pretended not to notice. I looked over at Sarah to see her reaction, but she was examining a broken fingernail and didn't even look up.

"So, Andrea," Marcie said, putting the brush away, "what kind of loot did you get in your stocking?"

Andrea seemed startled by the question. "Oh, nothing special. You know, bubble bath, things like that."

"No, I didn't mean actually in your stocking, silly. I mean what did your dad give you?"

"Richard? Oh, he just lets Maggie do the shopping for both of them. Clothes, mainly."

I could tell that Andrea wasn't too pleased with this conversation, but obviously I was the only one who noticed, because Marcie the Mouth went on.

"I don't mean Richard, I mean the one in California. What'd he send you?"

I couldn't stand it any longer. "Marcie! That's a very personal question." Then I added, "Anyway, you didn't tell us what your father sent you."

Yeah, I know, that's just as rude, but I couldn't help

114

myself. Anyway, I don't think you should have to worry about respecting the feelings of someone who doesn't seem to have any feelings in the first place.

"Fran, the reason I haven't *told* you is because I haven't received it yet." She was using her how-can-you-be-so-obtuse tone of voice. She does that a lot when she's talking to me. "I was supposed to go for a visit, remember? He was being a real pest about my coming, but then it got put off. Anyway, I'll get my present when I go out there. Did I mention I might be going to New Jersey tomorrow?"

"No, you didn't," Sarah said.

"I bet you're looking forward to it," Andrea said.

"Well, it means a lot to my father to have me come, so I guess I am. He wanted me to stay with him, you know, but I chose to come to the Big Apple with Mom. Anyway, I guess I can stand being back in the old neighborhood for a few days," she said.

I was going to ask her what was so terrible about the old neighborhood, but the waitress came with our food, and nobody spoke while she set down our orders. Then we all got busy eating. The burgers tasted *so* good, and the hot chocolate was just right: hot, but not *too* hot. As we waited for the check, Marcie asked, "What're we going to do now?"

"Let's look in the windows along Fifth Avenue. We can walk uptown until we get to F.A.O. Schwarz," Sarah said. Sarah and I love to go to the famous toy store when we're downtown. Even though we're getting too big for most of the stuff, it's still a great place to browse.

As we left the restaurant, the four of us slung our ice skates over our shoulders and linked arms. We took up almost the entire sidewalk. People looked annoyed when they had to go around us, and several times we had to break the chain when somebody in a hurry just threatened to bulldoze through. The streets were packed with people, as they always are at this time of year. All the schools are closed, and I guess lots of people are in town visiting relatives. Everybody wants to see the stores decorated for the holidays, and the famous Christmas tree at Rockefeller Center. Most of the time, New York is just New York: The buildings are gray, the streets are kind of messy, and I have to be careful somebody doesn't steal my money. But on days like today, *I* was a tourist, too; and since the city was my home, I was very proud of it.

"Let's look at the jewelry!" Marcie said, as we came to Tiffany's at Fifty-seventh Street.

We went through the revolving doors and right past a guard who stared at us as if *daring* us to do something improper.

"Do you think he knows we don't have enough money to buy anything in this store?" Sarah asked.

"Most of the people who come in here probably don't have enough money," Andrea said, and there was a flicker of silence as we all stared at Andrea, each one of us probably thinking the same thing: Andrea was one of the ones who did.

She giggled self-consciously. "Don't look at me. I have about three bucks in my pocket."

That broke the tension, and we went up and down

on the elevator, looked in all the fancy showcases, and then revolved ourselves out through the fancy doors and onto Fifth Avenue again.

"That was fun," I said, as we waited at the corner of Fifty-seventh Street for the light. "Now on to something more our style."

"Yeah . . . teddy bears," Sarah said, and we all screamed as if that was absolutely the funniest thing we'd ever heard.

Tiffany's had been crowded, but F.A.O. Schwarz was a solid wall of people. We had to stand in line just to get through the front doors. Inside, as always, it was a wonderland of toys: giant pandas bigger than a man; dollhouses that you could walk through; dolls in satin and lace; intricate games; rainbow-colored toys that could teach a child to read, and count, and recognize colors. We stopped at the department where they sold dollhouse furniture and all the little accessories that go into dollhouses.

"It makes me wish I still had my dollhouse," Sarah said.

"What did you do with it?" I asked.

"Don't you remember? I gave it to my cousin Courtney last year."

"Oh, that's right. I still have mine, but it's shoved in the back of a closet."

"I left mine in our house in New Jersey," Marcie said.

I looked over at Andrea. "I don't remember—did you have one?"

She nodded. "It's upstairs," she said quietly.

Upstairs. She meant in the attic, where she kept all the things that were too plain or too shabby to be exhibited in the Fairchild house—all her possessions from before the divorce. Upstairs, where Andrea kept a special part of herself hidden.

We looked around some more, and then Sarah checked her watch.

"It's almost four. We'd better start home."

"Yeah," I agreed. "It'll be the pits if we get into the rush-hour traffic."

We made our way reluctantly out of the store, but not before each of us bought a souvenir. Sarah bought a tiny little teddy bear on roller skates, and Andrea bought the same teddy bear on a key chain. I bought a Santa Claus pen, and Marcie bought a miniature set of books—the sort you'd see in a dollhouse. That surprised me.

We stood all the way home on the bus, and it was just getting dark as we reached our street. That's the rule: home before dark.

"See you tomorrow," Sarah called as she and Marcie turned in at their building.

We all waved and went inside.

"Did you have fun?" I asked Andrea as we started upstairs without waiting for the elevator.

"I sure did. You kids are so lucky! You go *everywhere* by yourselves. I have to be driven here, picked up there. Gosh, it was fun just hopping on and off those buses. Thanks so much!"

"Don't thank me, I didn't do anything," I said, laughing. But I didn't really believe that was true.

Andrea lived in a mansion, but I lived in New York. I felt as if today I had done it all just for my friend's enjoyment: the store windows, the skating rink, the Christmas tree, the happy crowds. New York City was a fairyland, and it belonged to Fran Davies. This was the way I had dreamed it would be when Andrea came to visit. Except in my daydreams, there were only *three* of us linking arms, going up Fifth Avenue. . . .

14

I stood at the window and peered down at a street bathed in early morning sunlight. There was one person outside already. He was walking his dog, and he was carrying a "pooper scooper." I always wanted to have a dog, but now I'm glad we don't have one. If I had to clean up after it like the man was doing, I'd die.

I came back from the bathroom and checked the clock: 7:20. Andrea's blonde head was tucked under the covers, and I could hear her breathing nice and steadily. She probably wouldn't wake up for another hour. I got back into bed and lay there thinking about what we'd do today. Maybe we'd go and see the windows at Lord & Taylor. I wondered what Sarah and Marcie were going to do. Maybe Marcie was going to New Jersey. . . . No, that would be too good to be true. And Sarah didn't seem to be able to go anywhere without her. It was as if they were Siamese twins, joined at the hip. It used to be that way with Sarah and me. I started to feel sad again, but then I brightened: I had a new friend, sleeping right next to me. And whenever I felt sorry for myself, I thought about how lonely Andrea's life had been. So what if my folks fight a little, now and then? They're not divorced like Andrea's or Marcie's. Maybe I should try to like Marcie more. Maybe under that obnoxious exterior, she was really a lonely, lost soul. But the more I thought about it, the more I decided that under that obnoxious exterior, there was an obnoxious *interior*.

Andrea turned around in bed and stretched. "How long have you been awake?" she asked, glancing over at me.

"Not too long."

"I could sleep forever. What time is it?"

"Almost eight o'clock. You hungry?"

"I don't know yet."

"What d'you mean, you don't know yet?"

"I never know whether I'm hungry or not until I'm up for a while."

"I'm always hungry in the morning. If Mom doesn't cook me anything, I fix myself a bowl of cereal. I've been having a lot of cereal lately."

Andrea was lying on her stomach, with her head hanging over the side of the bed.

"You didn't have cereal yesterday morning. We had blueberry pancakes, remember?"

"Yeah, that's right."

"Mmm . . . they were so good. I sure miss your mother's cooking. Bertha cooks such plain food."

"Yeah, Mom's a good cook. But now that she's so busy with this catering business, we don't get as much of the good stuff as we used to."

"Well, that's the high price of success, I guess. Your stomach pays," she said, giggling, "for your mother's

121

success." There was a pause while Andrea pulled herself upright and sat on the edge of the bed. "What's Marcie's mother like?"

"What makes you ask?"

"Oh, I don't know. Just the way Marcie talked about her yesterday, I guess. She and your mom are good friends, huh?"

"No, they're not, Andrea!" I said. I knew I was showing too much annoyance, but I couldn't help myself. "Marcie's mom is . . . well, she talks funny, for one thing. And she's real . . . *militant,* that's the word my dad uses. She's always trying to talk people into doing things her way. You wouldn't believe how she was going to have Mom decorate our apartment."

"How?"

"With potato sacks."

"You're kidding. Is she a decorator?"

"No, she's a potter."

"A what?"

"I knew you'd say that. See, I'm not so dumb! A potter's somebody who makes things out of clay."

"So what do they have in common?"

"That's just it. *Nothing.* That gibberish about my mom getting out of prison. I wanted to sock her for that."

"She didn't mean it that way. She meant your mom was—"

"*Not* a cookie baker."

"That was funny!"

"Everything about that family is *funny,*" I said in disgust.

"You don't like Marcie, do you?"

"I hate her." We didn't say anything for a minute, and then I turned and looked at Andrea. "I don't know why I said that."

"Sure you do," Andrea said quietly, "because you hate her."

We laughed, but down deep inside, I felt as if something small and hard were forming in the pit of my stomach. I had disliked people before, sure, but when had I started really *hating* Marcie? It seems like really hating a person is something so strong and terrible, that you should notice it happening. It should almost *hurt*. Maybe that's why I felt afraid suddenly: I could be the one hurt by my feelings, not Marcie.

"Come on, let's see what's for breakfast," Andrea said.

When we came out to the kitchen, Mom was just getting her coat on. "Oh, I didn't know you two were awake. I'm sorry I can't fix you some breakfast, but I've got to get down to C.B.'s loft."

Andrea glanced over at me.

"Why are you going down there?" I asked.

"Oh, things are happening, Fran. C.B. feels very, very strongly that I should rent space where she does, in Greenwich Village. But I'm not sure. I have that offer from Joel Kirsten—you know, he has that shop on East Seventy-seventh Street?—and I promised I'd let him know the first of the year. It's very confusing." She sighed deeply as she struggled with her boots. "Anyway, your father's going to meet us down in the Village later this afternoon. Wish me luck," she said, and she blew kisses to both of us as she flew out the door.

We had just finished our cereal when Sarah called. It was funny—when she asked, "What'll we do today?" I had a mixed reaction. Part of me was glad, because that's the way it used to be all the time. But part of me was resentful that she was including herself in everything with Andrea and me.

"We're going down to see the Lord & Taylor windows. You want to come?"

"Okay. But Metcalfe's gone to New Jersey. So maybe you two want to go by yourselves?"

Again: Part of me was glad that Marcie was in New Jersey, but part of me was annoyed that Sarah *knew* that Marcie was in New Jersey, even before she called us. "No, no, Sarah," I said, "you can come." I was ashamed of myself for the feeling of power that saying those words gave me.

"Are you sure?"

"Of course I'm sure. Be downstairs about eleven."

By the time we got to Lord & Taylor, there was already a line of people waiting to look at the windows. It occurred to me that we were doing a lot of waiting in line during Andrea's visit, but that was Christmastime in New York for you.

The theme of the windows was "Christmas on Old Broadway." The first window was "Babes in Toyland, 1903." There were giant blocks, and toy soldiers and dolls. The next featured the famous actress Maude

Adams in a production of "Peter Pan at the Empire Theater in 1905." The scene was set in a theater lobby, with a uniformed doorman. Next was "The Ziegfeld Follies at the New Amsterdam Theater, Christmas, 1920s." There were gorgeous clothes in this one, and an orchestra playing. The last window had Ethel Barrymore headlining a revue at the "Palace Theater, Christmas, 1914." This was supposed to be outside on the sidewalk, and there was a horse, and a boy throwing a snowball, and an old-fashioned photographer. All the details were so real, and so beautiful, it was difficult to take in each scene before you felt you had to move along so other people could see.

When we were finished, we started walking up Fifth Avenue. There was a mime performing outside the New York Public Library, and we stopped to watch him for a while. As we started to leave, he followed us for a few steps, imitating Sarah's walk, then he went back to his audience. I pointed to the gigantic wreaths around the necks of the two stone lions that sit on either side of the library steps.

"Aren't they cute?" I asked Andrea.

She nodded. "You know, there's so much to see in New York, and you don't have to pay for any of it," she said.

Sarah was starting to say something in agreement when she spotted a wagon on the corner of Forty-second Street. "Hot pretzels!" she cried, hurrying over. The pretzel vendor was short and stocky, with a black mustache and a face that needed a shave. He wore a brown knitted cap pulled down over his ears, and he stomped his feet up and down to keep warm as he barked at customers.

"What'll it be, girls?"

"Who wants one?" Sarah said, fishing her wallet out of her bag.

"You go ahead. I don't want any. How about you, Andrea?"

Andrea looked curious. "I've never had one."

"What? You *have* led a sheltered life, haven't you! You've got to try one. Here," she said, rummaging in her bag for more money, "I'll treat."

"Oh no, that's okay, I'll pay for it," Andrea said, giving the man the money and taking her pretzel.

"Why don't we show Andrea the Trump Tower?" Sarah suggested.

"Good idea," I said, and we headed uptown to Fifty-sixth Street. "We passed it yesterday, but with all the crowds you probably didn't notice," I said to Andrea.

"Was that the place with the fancy uniformed doormen?"

"Yeah, that was it."

We walked along in silence for a few minutes, then Andrea said, "I wonder how Marcie's doing in New Jersey."

I had to pull my attention away from a little old man whose overcoat was completely covered with campaign buttons. It was so heavy he could hardly walk. "I'm sure she's doing fine," I said, looking at her.

"I wonder what it's like to have your folks fighting over you," Sarah said.

"I don't think they're actually fighting over her," I said. I had to bite my tongue so I wouldn't add, "*Who would fight over Marcie?*" I had to remember she was somebody's kid, and I guess you'd feel differently if you had actually given birth to her. I imagine when she was born, she didn't make a grand entrance wearing dangling earrings, a frizzy perm, and six labels attached to her body.

"I think they are," Sarah continued. "She told me once that when her mom 'split'—that's what they called the divorce—her dad wanted her to stay with him out in New Jersey, but her mother wanted her to 'grow to womanhood in a supportive atmosphere.' I think that's kind of *neat*."

I looked at Sarah like she was losing her marbles. Luckily we had arrived at the entrance to the Trump building, so I didn't get a chance to pursue the subject.

Trump Tower is, as you might guess from its name, a vertical shopping mall, paved in gold. You can look up, practically forever, and see balconies with shops and plants and lots of gleaming gold and glass. And down in the center of it all, there's a fancy place to eat. My folks think it's too glitzy, but Sarah and I like it. When we're grown-up, we're going to do all our shopping there and then stop for lunch that we'll pay for with our American Express Gold Cards. We planned that last year, one day when we were really bored. As we stood looking around at everything, I remembered that, and I wondered if Sarah remembered it, too.

But all she said was, "I don't know about you, but I'm ready to hit the bus."

We walked slowly over to Sixth Avenue and then raced to jump on a bus that was just lurching to a stop on the corner. We had to stand all the way uptown, bumping against each other every time the bus stopped. By the time we got to the apartment, I was beginning to regret not buying a pretzel.

"I'm famished," I said to Andrea as we ran up the stairs. "I wonder what's for dinner."

"Whatever it is, I'm sure it'll be great," she said.

But as we opened the door, it was clear that whatever we were having wasn't on the stove yet. The apartment was dark and empty. I switched on the hall light and then a lamp in the living room. I always get the creeps coming in when it's getting dark and the apartment is empty. I was glad that Andrea was with me.

"Anybody home?" I yelled, knowing that it was a stupid thing to do. If anybody was home, would they be sitting silently in the semi-darkness?

"I guess they'll be in any minute," I said. "I thought they'd be home by now."

Andrea looked at me. "You know, Fran, it's not unusual for nobody to be home yet. It's not that late. My parents don't get home until eight most of the time. If it wasn't for Bertha, I'd come home to an empty house almost every day."

"Oh, I know," I said. "I guess I'm just spoiled. Mom's always been here, or if she's not, Dad usually is. You know, with him being a teacher, he gets home early lots of times."

Suddenly there were footsteps coming down the

hall, and voices, loud and querulous. A key turned in the lock, and my parents were home, marching down the hall like an invading army, letting the door slam shut behind them. Once inside, they didn't speak, and their silence was louder than any screaming. Mom forced a tight little smile when she saw us.

"Hello, girls. How was your day? Have fun?" She hung her coat in the hall closet without waiting for an answer and went into the kitchen.

Dad threw his coat and hat on a chair and took the newspaper, which had been tucked under his arm, into the living room. I glanced nervously over at Andrea.

"Let's go into your room," she said softly.

We did, and as we switched on the ceiling light and closed the door, I could hear my mother going into one of her dish-rattling routines in the kitchen. What had happened to make them so mad? Was it something to do with C.B.'s loft?

Andrea had sprawled across the bed, so I took the floor. It was times like this that I wished I had my own television. We could turn on a rerun of "Gilligan's Island" or an old movie or, if nothing else was on, the news. Instead, we just lay there, letting silence fill up the room.

They tried to whisper, but the words came out in such short, explosive gasps that even though we couldn't hear what they were saying, it was obvious they were having an argument.

I was so embarrassed, I couldn't look at Andrea. I looked instead around my bedroom. This was the kind of furniture Andrea had up in her attic. Oh, hers was more babyish, but it was ordinary stuff like this, things that wouldn't look right in her bedroom in Merriweather. Was that what I was coming to?

I could see it all now. I'd be living in a mansion. Just Mom and me . . . and her new husband, the sausage king.

"What do you think?" Andrea asked me, giving the bright red noisemaker another quick spin. It made a loud, crackling sound.

"That one's fine," I said.

"And hats, we'll need some hats." She darted down the aisle and chose a bright pink pointed one for herself, a blue one for me, and a gold one for Sarah. "I still wish we could try these out," she said, fingering the packages of brightly wrapped horns lumped on the counter. "This is going to be the best New Year's Eve ever! Aren't you excited?"

I tried to force a smile. "Yeah," I said.

"What's the matter? You still upset about your folks?"

For a second, I could feel tears springing to my eyes, and I fought them back. I couldn't cry. Not right out here, in public! "I'm not upset," I lied. "Why should I be upset?" I followed her along the counter while she picked up a package of streamers.

"I guess we don't need these," she said. "We're not going to decorate the McAuliffes' apartment, are we?" she asked.

131

I shook my head. "Why should I be upset?" I repeated.

She stopped and looked at me. "You seem to be upset a lot these days, Fran. I've noticed it in little things that have happened. I'll have to give you some of Andrea's handy-dandy coping tricks," she said, laughing as we made our way to the cashier. "If your folks are breaking up, Fran, that's a shame, but there's nothing much you can do about it, you know? And you'll just make yourself miserable if you think about it all the time."

I stopped moving and just stared at her. "Andrea, my folks aren't breaking up! What would make you think they are? Just because they have a little argument . . ."

"Fine, great. Then there's nothing to worry about."

"Do you think they are? Do you?" Because, of course, Andrea would know. Andrea was an expert on parents fighting, I wasn't.

"I don't know, Fran," she said seriously. "I just notice that they're different. I only met your dad that one time, remember, during the summer, when we went for pizza?" I nodded, my throat suddenly feeling tight at the memory. That seemed so long ago. A different Fran, and different parents. "I remember he was so nice. I loved hearing him talk about his work. It reminded me so much of my dad."

"So you think he's changed?"

She squeezed my hand as we left the store, as if she was afraid she'd said something bad.

"Just a little bit. He's more serious."

132

"And grumpy. Honestly, Andrea, the way he was when you saw him last summer, that's the way he used to be all the time. Now he's mad all the time. And mostly at Mom."

"Your mom's different, too, you know."

I let out a huge sigh. Strange as it may seem, I felt relieved. It wasn't crazy Fran's imagination. Mom was different, Dad was different.

"I know she is, but it's C.B.'s fault. If only she and that stupid daughter of hers had stayed in New Jersey. They've changed everything. They've ruined my whole life!"

We had come to the candy store, and Andrea started inside. I followed her.

"I thought we should get some candy to take with us tonight," she said.

"That's a good idea." I was glad that Sarah had invited us to baby-sit with her. We were going to have our own New Year's Eve party. We loaded up on Kit Kats, Gummy Bears, and Hershey's bars, and came back outside.

"I think you're exaggerating a little," Andrea said as we waited at the corner for the light to change.

"About what?"

"About C.B. and Marcie ruining your life."

"I am not!" Again, I felt close to tears. I realized I needed to talk to someone. I've always been able to talk to Sarah when something was bothering me, but now she gets this really hurt look on her face if I make even the tiniest nasty remark about Marcie. And it used to be, if I had a fight with Sarah, I could go to

Mom, and she'd understand. But now that she was trying to cook her way to the top, she never seemed to have any time. "Do you know how my folks are spending New Year's Eve this year?" I asked Andrea.

She shook her head. "No, how?"

"They're not, that's how," I said. Andrea looked a little confused, so I went on. "Every year they spend it in the same way. It started the year they were married. There was a big snowstorm, and they were supposed to go to a party, and they couldn't go, but they got dressed up anyway and stayed home and had champagne and watched an old movie on television." I paused for breath. "And so now, that's what they do every year. My dad still has the same velvet smoking jacket he wore then. The only time he wears it is on New Year's Eve. We always kid him about it."

"So?"

"So, this year my dad's going to be home alone because Mom has to help cater the Sheffield party!"

"Well, that's her *business*, Fran."

"No, it isn't. I mean, she was just going to make a few hors d'oeuvres for people, but C.B. turned her into the Catering Queen of the West Side. Those Sheffield people are giving a big party. Mom wouldn't even have known about it, but C.B. heard about it and got Mom involved."

"Fran, you've got to realize that if your mom didn't want to do all this she wouldn't be doing it. C.B.'s just helping your mom, giving her a little push."

"I'd like to give *her* a little push. If Mom chooses the Village over that Kirsten job, Dad's gonna have a fit."

"Well, Fran, that's between your mom and dad."

"Okay, so maybe that is. But what about Marcie? I mean, she stole Sarah away from me!" I knew, as soon as I said it, that it sounded really strange. I guess it was all coming out of me at once: all the anger and frustration of these past few months, when nothing was supposed to change, but everything did. I had the fleeting thought that it was a good thing Andrea lived in Merriweather, so there was no chance of her going around school saying how weird I was. But I knew Andrea would never do that. After all, I had sat with her in her attic, and she had shared some of her most private feelings. "I guess you think I'm silly," I said.

"Of course not," she said as we came to my building and went upstairs. "But I don't know why you're so mad at everyone for having new friends. You've got a new friend, haven't you?"

"I do? Who?"

"Me! What am I, a cocker spaniel?"

I gave her a shove as we reached the apartment door, and we went in laughing.

Andrea hadn't really given me much sympathy, but somehow I felt better about everything. It's like all those articles say, you should talk about your troubles. Andrea was a really good friend, and that gave me an idea.

We had flopped down in my room with the party stuff, and I went over and took something out of the drawer. It was the little velvet jewelry box that I had made for Sarah. It wasn't really perfect—there was a little ragged edge on the inside—but if you didn't look

135

too closely, and when it was filled with jewelry, it would look pretty good.

"Here," I said, handing it to Andrea, "I want you to have this."

Andrea looked startled. "What is it?"

"It's a jewelry box that I was going to give to Sarah as an extra Christmas present, but I want you to have it instead. You're a better friend than she is."

Andrea examined it for a minute. "It's really nice," she said. Then she looked up at me. "But I can't take it."

"You don't like it," I said.

"That's not it. Of course I do. But you should give it to Sarah." I shook my head. "No, listen to me, Fran. Giving me this means you're giving up on your friendship with Sarah, and that would be terrible after all these years. Give her a little time, Fran. Be nice to Marcie. Then you can all be friends."

I took back the box. "It wouldn't work," I said.

"Try it. What do you have to lose? If you *don't* try, you could lose your best friend."

I thought about that for a moment. I'd do anything not to lose Sarah's friendship. But if she liked Marcie better than me, if she had already chosen her, what could I do? I'd always be a tagalong, butting in where I wasn't welcome. And pretending to like Marcie would be so phony. *Give me one good reason to like Marcie Metcalfe,* I wanted to say to Andrea. But I didn't say it. Instead, I put the velvet box back in the drawer.

Mom called us into dinner then. We were eating early because she had to get to the Sheffield party.

"Will you be home in time to bring in the New Year with Dad?" I asked casually as I scraped the plates.

My mother didn't look at me, but I knew, I just knew, that my dad was listening for her answer.

"I don't know, Fran," she said quietly. "I'm going to try."

We got to Sarah's just as her parents were leaving. Mrs. McAuliffe was all dressed up in a lacy black dress, and she had that giddy look that grown-ups get on New Year's Eve. We told them to have a good time, and as soon as the door closed, we checked the kitchen.

"We've got Cheetos, potato chips and onion dip, Hawaiian Punch, and Eskimo Pies," Sarah announced.

"And we brought these," I said, opening the bag of candy for her to see.

"Great! Let me get Benjamin into bed. Turn on the television."

We settled down and watched "Dynasty," and then "Hotel." Then something called "Rockin' into the New Year" came on.

At eleven ten, Mrs. McAuliffe called to check on Benjamin. By a quarter to twelve, we had eaten all the Cheetos, all the potato chips and dip, and had drunk most of the Hawaiian Punch. "Rockin' into the New Year" was really bad, and we were all getting pretty tired. But I was thinking how nice it was not having Marcie Metcalfe around. Andrea didn't intrude on the friendship between Sarah and me, she added to it. Why couldn't Sarah see the difference and realize what a nuisance Marcie was?

"Did I tell you about meeting Marcie's mom in the hall today?" Sarah asked. I shook my head, feeling guilty, as if Sarah could tell what I had been thinking. "She says that Marcie's having a super time back in New Jersey. Isn't that a hoot, after the way she ragged on the place? I guess it was being back with Tricia that did it."

"Who's Tricia?" I asked.

"Oh, Tricia's this really good friend Marcie had in New Jersey. Gosh, when she first came here, that's all I heard: Tricia this and Tricia that. Of course, I was driving her crazy with Fran this and Fran that. When she stopped talking about Tricia so much, I thought maybe she'd forgotten her. But I should have known better. You don't forget a friend."

"You don't?" I said.

"Of course not! What a question, Fran Davies! We didn't forget each other, did we?" she asked, "and after all, you were—"

"I know, I know," I said, "I was away all summer."

"Anyway, her mom says she's not really looking forward to coming back to New York. Can you imagine? And I thought she was so sophisticated."

"I don't know, Sarah, how sophisticated is someone who's still buying things for her old dollhouse?" Andrea asked.

I turned and stared at Andrea. Why hadn't I thought of that?

"You know, I meant to ask her about those books," Sarah said. "Anyway, she's going to spend the summer out there with her dad. That's what they've agreed

on, for now. It must be so *confusing* to live like that."
Then she added, "Oh, I'm sorry, Andrea, I didn't
mean—"

"That's okay," she said. "Hey, look at the television. They're starting to count down!"

We watched the ball descend from the tower in
Times Square, and then Andrea and Sarah and I ran
over to the window and blew our horns and yelled
"Happy New Year!" just like the people on the television were doing.

After a few minutes, they went into the kitchen to
get the Eskimo Pies, but I stayed at the window, listening to the happy sounds of the New Year fading out
all around the neighborhood. So Marcie had left a
good friend back in New Jersey . . . and she'd even
missed her. Maybe Marcie Metcalfe was human, after
all. Could it be she laughed all the time only when I
was around? I felt strange. It was like the feeling I'd
had at Andrea's last summer, when I knew I didn't
envy her the carousel horse any longer. The feeling of
relief you get when you know you don't have to be
mad anymore.

It was a brand new year. Dad always says that gives
you a whole new start on things.

"Sarah," I said, turning around, "why don't we call
Marcie and wish her a Happy New Year?"

At first, Sarah just looked surprised. Then she
looked pleased.

"You mean it? Oh, wait, I don't know her number."

"We can get it from Information. Do you know her
father's name?"

"George."

"Come on, let's try it," I said. "Maybe we'll even wake her up!"

It was easy to get the number, but we didn't wake her up. She was watching "Rockin' into the New Year" with her dad. We all took turns yelling "Happy New Year!" into the phone, and when she said she'd be back tomorrow, I heard myself say "Great" before I handed the phone to Andrea.

Things quieted down a lot after that. We watched an old movie and ate the Eskimo Pies and some of the candy. The McAuliffes came home about one thirty, and Mr. McAuliffe walked Andrea and me back to my building.

When we opened the door, it was very quiet. I wasn't sure who was home yet, but I was too tired to care, and I was so sleepy I could hardly see. That's probably why it was Andrea who spotted the champagne bottle on the table in the living room.

But I was the one who noticed the smoking jacket thrown over the chair.

"I still don't think she's a particularly terrific person,"
I said, spitting toothpaste into the sink as I glanced up
at Andrea in the bathroom mirror.

"Fran, nobody's saying she's Mother Teresa. Just
give a little, for your own sake. You didn't like me in
the beginning, did you? Don't deny it!"

I felt myself blush as I wiped my mouth on a towel.
"Who told you that?"

"Nobody had to tell me. You used to have this
really stricken look on your face if you even had to pass
me in the hall, don't you remember?"

"Well, that's because I thought . . . never mind."

"You thought what?"

I giggled at the memory. "Promise you won't be
mad or hurt or anything?"

"Promise."

"I thought you were the town snot."

"*What?*"

"Well, you weren't. So it doesn't matter."

"Gee, then you'd think you'd have been nicer to
Marcie. I mean, you should realize by now what a
lousy judge of character you are!"

I threw the towel at her, and we went in to have breakfast.

Everybody seemed to be pretty cheerful this morning. I didn't say anything about the champagne bottle, but I noticed it wasn't on the table anymore. The smoking jacket was still lying on the chair, so I knew the whole thing wasn't the result of my one-thirty-in-the-morning imagination.

"What time does your train leave, Andrea?" Dad asked.

"Five after three."

"Oh, then we've got plenty of time. We'll leave here a little after two."

"Do you want to go for a walk?" I asked Andrea. "I haven't shown you Riverside Drive yet."

"Sure," she said, and we excused ourselves and got dressed.

"Do you really think I'm a bad judge of character?" I asked Andrea as we walked along the top of the park, breathing in the crisp, cold air. It had snowed a little overnight, and the snow covered the earth like the sprinkling of sugar on a cookie.

"I don't know, Fran. It seems to me you shouldn't judge people at all. But maybe I've just had more practice not doing that. You've never had to bother."

We walked in silence for a few minutes, and I thought about that. I guess getting somebody new for a father, especially somebody like Richard, would make you a more tolerant person. Maybe things had been so nice and normal for the Davies family that I wasn't in train-

142

ing for change, or tolerance, or compromise. "Did I ever really thank you for telling Brenda to be nice to me?" Andrea said, changing the subject.

"I never told her to—"

"Oh, Fran, come on, I know you did. That's okay, it worked! All I needed was a chance to get to know those guys. I know more kids at school, I'm invited more places, things are really a lot less lonely for me. So the next time you come up, we probably won't be visiting the attic." I looked at her. "I don't need that anymore. Those are memories, Fran, and I'm beginning to like it fine right where I am now. I don't have to keep remembering so much."

I reached over and gave her a hug. "I'm so glad, Andrea."

And I *was* glad, not only for Andrea, but for myself, too. Maybe that meant I wasn't a hopelessly insensitive clod after all. But then again, maybe I was, because it was at that exact moment that my sixth sense failed me once again.

By the time I realized that someone was running up behind me, it was too late. As I turned around, Charlie Bidwell flung a handful of snow in my face. I screamed, and Andrea giggled.

"I'll get you for that!" I yelled after him as he took off with his friends along the top of the Drive.

"Boy, you're sure starting the new year right!" Andrea said as I tried to wipe the snow off my face with my glove.

I grinned. "Yeah," I said.

"I'll write to you tomorrow," Andrea promised as we waited in Grand Central station for her train.

"And I'll write to you tomorrow," I answered.

Then we both laughed.

I was glad that my father and I got seats together on the bus going back uptown. I had that letdown feeling I sometimes get when something I've looked forward to is all over. I had enjoyed Andrea's visit so much. It was almost like having a sister.

My father didn't speak much at first, but I didn't get the feeling I'd had the past few weeks, that he was mad about something or that he didn't want to talk. So I said, "Did you have a nice New Year's Eve?"

He looked over at me with a confused frown, as if I had interrupted his thoughts. He does that sometimes, and we always call him the absentminded professor when he does, but I didn't say anything today.

"Yes, Fran, we did."

I noticed he said *we*. I hadn't asked him about Mom, but he included her anyway.

"What time did Mom get home?" I asked, trying desperately to sound casual and wondering if I'd regret even bringing up the subject. But I kept thinking about the smoking jacket and the champagne. I hadn't imagined them.

"About midnight," he said, still sounding distracted.

"What are you thinking about?" I asked.

He looked over at me again, but this time he smiled.

"I'm making my New Year's resolutions," he said.

"What are they?" I asked.

144

"Aren't you inquisitive! I'm not telling. If I did, you'd know all my imperfections."

"I never thought of it that way. But I'm making some, too. How about if I tell you mine, and then you tell me yours?"

"Nope."

"Come on, that's not fair. How about telling me just a couple of them?"

"How many do you think I'm making? I haven't been that much of a reprobate."

"A what?"

"Look it up."

We came to our stop and got off the bus. "I'm going to be more tolerant and not judge people so much," I blurted out.

"That sounds like an excellent resolution, New Year's or not."

"So?"

"What do you mean, 'So?' "

"So what's yours?"

"I don't have to tell you."

"But *I* told *you!*"

"Okay, okay. I guess my resolution is a lot like yours, Fran. Maybe we're coming from the same place this New Year's."

"Huh?"

"We live in the same house, with the same person, one who's been undergoing a kind of . . . identity crisis. I could have been a lot more supportive than I've been, but I'm turning over a new leaf."

"Good. So am I. Do you know what she's decided

145

about the job?" It seemed so funny to be calling Mom *she* and talking to Dad about her like she was a homework problem we couldn't solve. At the mention of the job, he relaxed even more, and he grinned. "She's taking Joel Kirsten's offer. We talked it over last night, but it was her own decision."

"I'm so glad! I can't stand that C.B." It was the first time I'd actually said that to Dad, but I was pretty sure he felt the same way.

"Well, Fran, I guess that's what our New Year's resolutions are all about, right? *We* don't have to like her. She's Mom's friend, not ours. But we shouldn't be unpleasant about it. Mom's making some changes in her life, and most of them will be very nice. Maybe she just needs somebody a little crazy like C.B. to rev her up."

We had gotten to our building, and Dad held the squeaky metal door open for me.

"We're gonna be terrific, Dad, you'll see."

"Tolerance," he said, looking at me, and he winked.

"Tolerance," I echoed as we went upstairs to the apartment.

After dinner, I got a chance to talk to Mom in the kitchen.

"You're going to work for Joel Kirsten, right?"

"How did you know? Oh, your dad told you."

"Is that all right? It wasn't a secret, was it?"

"Of course not, Fran. Why would I keep it a secret?"

146

"I don't know, I guess that was stupid. Are you happy about it?"

Mom paused for a moment, then turned around and looked at me. "Yes, Fran, I'm *very* happy about it. I feel relieved. It'll be so much better for me at this point. I'll have regular hours, and I won't have to work out of this small kitchen. And I'll be learning. You know, I'm not as original as I thought. I'm a neophyte, Fran."

"A what?"

"A beginner. I'll learn a lot working with Joel. He's very successful, and he seems like a very nice person."

"Does that mean you're going to get rid of *that?*" I asked, pointing to THE AWAKENED COOKIE BAKER sign, which still hung over the sink.

Mom looked surprised. "Why would I want to get rid of that? It's cute. And I think it's significant. It's special to me."

I was sorry I had asked. "Then you're still friends with—"

"With C.B.? Of course. Why not?"

"No, no, I'm glad," I said hurriedly. "She's probably your *best* friend now, huh?"

Mom seemed to think that was very funny. "*Best* friend, Fran? I haven't thought in terms of best friends since I was in high school. No, that's not true. . . . Claudia Simpson is still my best fr— Anyway, Fran, for goodness sakes, C.B. is just a fun kind of person who's given me some wind in my sails when I needed it. How good a friend she is, I don't know. Does it matter?"

"Not a bit," I said. And I meant it.

Mom could be friends with C.B., and I could be friends with Marcie. And Sarah could be friends with Marcie, but Sarah could also be friends with me. And I could be friends with Andrea, but I could also be friends with Sarah. This sharing business was easy once you got the hang of it.

There's only one problem. I don't think this plan is going to work once we get to Charlie Bidwell.

17.

Dear Andrea,

It's nine o'clock, and I'm supposed to be in bed, but I'm wide awake, so I thought I'd write to you. Only two weeks late!

I wanted to thank you so much for coming for a visit. I got your thank-you note, and I'm glad you had a good time, too.

I thought you'd like to know that I gave the velvet jewelry box to Sarah after all, and guess what? She gave me the green heart that I had wanted for my birthday! So I think things are going to be okay after all. Even Marcie seems to be a lot nicer since she came back from New Jersey. But I know now that things keep changing, and they're not always going to be the same, so I'll need my good friend Andrea around.

I hope you have a super year. I have a feeling this is going to be a really wonderful one for me. And honestly, Andrea, it has nothing to do with the fact that Marcie's going to be away all summer.

Love from your friend,
Fran

149